Arkansas Smith

Arkansas Smith: the name was legend. Once he had been a Texas Ranger, but now he was something else entirely. Some said he was an outlaw, a killer of men and a fast draw. Others claimed he was a kind of special lawman, dispensing frontier justice across the West and bringing law to the lawless.

Arkansas Smith arrives in Red Rock looking for those who shot and left his friend for dead. He vows to leave no stone unturned in his quest to bring the gunmen to justice and, soon, those who go against him must face the legendary fast draw that helped tame the West.

By the same author

The Tarnished Star

Arkansas Smith

Jack Martin

A Black Horse Western

ROBERT HALE · LONDON

ISBN 978-0-7090-8889-9

Robert Hale Limited
Clerkenwell House
Clerkenwell Green
London EC1R 0HT

www.halebooks.com

To Anthony Brannan – pals!

Typeset by
Derek Doyle & Associates, Shaw Heath
Printed and bound in Great Britain by
CPI Antony Rowe, Chippenham and Eastbourne

ONE

Arkansas Smith carefully guided the sorrel down the steep incline that led into the valley. His heart was hammering in his chest and he wanted to spur the horse forward, but it was too dangerous and he had to lean back in the saddle. Carefully, with each step, he took his time for both his own and the horse's safety.

Below, perfectly positioned besides the stream that snaked around the valley, the small cabin looked deserted, its door hanging on rawhide hinges and blowing in the evening breeze, the windows smashed. Outside, fences had been torn down and whatever cattle the enclosures had contained had been run off or stolen.

It didn't look good and it seemed to take an age for the sorrel to negotiate the tricky terrain and reach the foot of the valley. Then Arkansas immediately sent the horse into a gallop. He reached the cabin and tethered the sorrel to the remains of a fence post before removing his Spencer from its boot, drawing his Colt and going inside.

Immediately the stench hit him like a tangible thing – the sweet cloying aroma of charred wood, the offensive perfume of urine and a putrid mixture of something far more unpleasant. It took a moment for Arkansas's eyes to adjust to the gloom and for several seconds he stood there motionless, peering at the mess around him.

The place had been ransacked. The furniture, such as it was, had been overturned, papers were strewn all over the place, and there had been an attempt to set the place on fire, only it had burnt itself out but not before damaging a large section of the back wall and part of the roof.

'Hello? Anyone here?' Arkansas said, not expecting an answer and not getting one.

There was a chair in the corner of the room and it was threadbare, feathers escaping from a large rip in the cushion. Another chair had been kicked over and one of its legs had been charred in the fire. There was a wooden table, made from packing crates and it had been toppled over and one of the legs snapped in two. Newspapers, glass and the odd dime novel were strewn over the floor.

'Will,' Arkansas called out, but again there was nothing in reply.

It was a two-room building and Arkansas carefully stepped over the wreckage and made his way to the door at the rear of the room. His hand paused on the handle and, keeping the Colt pointed directly in front of him, he pushed and allowed the door to swing inwards. Like the outer door it too had rawhide hinges, which screeched in protest as the door opened.

He saw the motionless figure on the floor, face down, and he knew immediately that it was Will. He propped his rifle against the wall and then went and bent to the man, rolling him over. The man had been gut shot and the wound was surrounded by congealed blood. Arkansas felt for a heartbeat, found one but very faint, almost imperceptible.

Will was alive but only just.

'Will,' Arkansas said. It's me, Ark. Can you hear me?'

There was no response from the man and Arkansas quickly ran out of the cabin and took a cooking pot from his saddle-bags. He ran to the stream and filled the pot and then took it back into the house.

'Come on,' Arkansas said as he dipped a clean bandanna in the water and carefully moistened his friend's lips. For a moment there was no reaction but then the man moaned and his tongue licked at the cool water. Maybe he wasn't as badly hurt as it had first appeared.

'You're gonna be fine, Will.' Arkansas murmured, knowing that his words would sound hollow to his friend. He had known William McCord for a great many years; they had served in the Texas Rangers together and seen much action. Side by side, they had fought Indians, outlaws and Mexican raiders.

Platitudes were useless: Will would know what his chances were.

Carefully Arkansas lifted his friend and placed him

on the small mattress in the corner of the room. He used the water first to wash the man's face and then he went to work on the wound. He tore the man's shirt open and looked at the ugly purple bruising where the bullet had entered. There was no exit wound and when Arkansas gently prodded he felt the bullet, lodged in the thick flesh of the stomach. He didn't think the wound itself was enough to be fatal, but his friend was in a bad way and infection would probably finish the job that the bullet had started.

He cleaned the area surrounding the entry point, taking care as he rubbed in the immediate vicinity of the injury and then went outside to get some fresh water. He returned a moment later and when he examined his friend he found he was fast asleep and his breathing was better, more even. It was a hopeful sign and Arkansas mopped the man's forehead down and then soaked his lips once more.

'You always were an ornery critter,' Arkansas told him. 'Come on, it'll take more than a bullet to finish off William McCord.'

The man didn't stir and Arkansas decided to let him sleep while he got a fire going and boiled some water to once again clean the gut wound before dressing it.

He left the room, closed the door gently behind him and quickly set a fire in the cast-iron stove. He used some of the wood from a broken chair and looked around and located some goose grease in a pan in the far corner. He smeared it thickly over the wood and took a match to it – the fire caught immediately and Arkansas fed it with some paper and old cloth from the floor and within minutes it was burning away well.

He threw some more wood on and closed the stove door.

'I don't think the bullet's gone in deep enough to do any real damage,' Arkansas said. 'You always did have the dandiest luck. I need to get you to a doc though. It'll have to come out.'

'Hurt enough going in,' Will said.

Dawn had risen over the valley and was illuminating the interior of the cabin. Dust danced in the rays of light that came through the broken windows and gave the place an oppressive atmosphere. In the brilliance of day the place looked as if a herd of buffalo had stampeded through.

Will had spent a comfortable night and this was the first time he had regained consciousness for anything more than a few minutes. Some of the colour had returned to his cheeks and, although gravely ill, he certainly looked a heck of a lot better.

'I'm on fire,' Will said.

'That's to be expected,' Arkansas replied. 'That slug in you wouldn't have gone in clean and it's sitting in your guts now causing all sorts of infection.' He mopped the man's forehead with a damp cloth and then smiled. 'You've come this far. We're going to get out of this.'

Will nodded and motioned weakly for another drink of water.

'I thought I was dead and seeing a ghost when I saw you hovering over me. I heard you'd been hanged down in Reno,' he said. 'It's been a long time.'

'A lot of folk seem to have heard that one,' Arkansas muttered, and handed his friend a tin cup but only allowed him a mouthful before taking it away. Too much, too quickly could do more harm than good.

'Who did this?' asked Arkansas, placing the cup on the floor between his feet.

'Rustlers,' Will told him. 'I heard them riding up and went out and then all hell broke loose.'

'When?'

'Yesterday.' A puzzled expression crossed Will's face. 'I'm not sure. I don't think I know.'

'Judging by the wound,' Arkansas said. 'I'd say two days ago. The blood's congealed and stopped you from bleeding to death.'

'I'll live,' Will replied. 'Just long enough to see them turkeys who gunned me down swinging at the end of a rope.'

Arkansas looked at the man and nodded. He had known him a great many years and was forever in his debt. They had served in the Rangers together and, although some twenty years separated them by age, the two men had hit it off at once. Will, the elder of the two, had taken the young Arkansas under his wing and taught him the ways of the Texas Rangers. The older man had saved his life more times than Arkansas cared to recall.

'They took your stock,' Arkansas told him. 'The

corral's been busted open. Whatever you had in there's clean gone. And they've taken this place apart, obviously looking for any money you might have tucked away.'

Will nodded and then coughed up a thin trickle of blood. 'I was down to my last fifty dollars and as for stock – weren't more than a few horses. I guess I was never going to make it ranching.'

Arkansas smiled. All his life Will had been a wandering man, too restless to stop in one place for too long. It was what had made him so good as a Texas Ranger, but ever since the he had turned fifty, he had been talking about getting himself some land, building a life in one place and sticking there. Too many years of constant wandering, fighting one campaign after another, would eventually affect most men in the same way, making them revaluate their lives. It made them yearn for a domesticity they had never known and only heard of in tales told around a camp-fire. Trouble was if they ever found it they would discover it too tame for their liking.

'Fifteen years a Ranger can give a man a case of wanderlust,' Arkansas said and offered Will the cup. He had only served six years himself, but all the same their ways were in his blood. He, too, would get that restless urge if he felt the grass growing beneath his feet. It had been a long time, however, since either man had ridden as a Ranger but each would keep their ways. Once a Ranger, always a Ranger.

Will took another sip and then winced as the slug inside him sent a fresh wave of pain through his nervous system. 'Wouldn't mind betting that bastard Lance is behind this.'

'Lance?' Arkansas asked.

Will nodded weakly but before he could speak further his eyes closed and once again he fell into a deep feverish sleep.

TWO

Later Arkansas thought he'd take a ride around, see if he could recover any of his friend's stock. You never know, a few might have broken free of the rustlers and wandered off into the wilderness. Although the town of Red Rock was only a few miles yonder, this was still a wild country with plenty of open spaces that stretched for miles and miles without any signs of civilization.

First though, the most pressing matter was getting the slug out of Will – it wasn't in too deeply and Arkansas believed it had missed the major organs and was lodged in the fatty flesh of the outer stomach. Will had been incredibly lucky, but Arkansas didn't think that luck would hold if he went probing about with his knife to remove the slug.

No, it had to come out but it needed the skilled hands of a doctor.

While he waited for his friend to wake, he set about tidying the place up a little. He righted the toppled furniture, fixed the table leg and placed boards over the broken windows. They kept some of the light out but they also stopped some of the heat escaping. Keeping the place warm was mighty important and would help sweat Will's fever out of him.

He found a pearl-handled dagger beneath a broken chair and, guessing it must have be thrown there when the place was ransacked, he placed it on the upturned Folgers crate that acted as a dresser in the bedroom. It was a handsome-looking knife, with a seven-inch blade and silver trim sunk into the pearl handle. It had felt perfectly balanced in Arkansas's hand. Will was especially skilled with knives and the piece was typical of the ornamental but at the same time practical weapons he usually favoured.

Arkansas was putting some more wood onto the stove when he heard his friend cry out. He turned on his feet and ran back into the bedroom.

Will was awake and he looked ghastly. His sweaty face had a yellow pallor and his eyes were bloodshot. The fever had him in its vice-like grip and Arkansas knew that the bullet had to come out quickly if his friend had any hope of survival. He needed to get him to a doctor but moving him could kill him. There was no wagon here and there was no way Will would be able to ride. Even in the back of a cart or wagon there would be too much jostling about.

'How far's town?' Arkansas asked.

'About five, maybe six miles south,' Will said, weakly. 'My mouth feels dry.'

Arkansas filled the cup with fresh water from the jug he'd placed on the makeshift dresser and placed it

14

gently on his friend's lips. He lifted it slightly so the man could take gentle sips.

'I reckon I could be there and back in not more than a couple of hours,' Arkansas said. 'Bring the doctor out to you.'

'Cooter,' Will said, and then fell silent for a moment while he gritted his teeth against a fresh wave of pain. 'Doctor Cooter. He's over fond of the whiskey, but he's a good man.'

Arkansas took the makings from his shirt and rolled a quirly. He stuck it in his friend's mouth, lit it and allowed him to take a small drag before smoking it himself.

'Our best chance,' Arkansas said, presently, 'is for me to go fetch this Cooter fellow and bring him here. Will you be OK while I'm gone?'

'I can look after myself,' Will said, annoyed. And for a brief moment he seemed to be his old self, his eyes blazing with inner strength. But in truth he was weak, too weak to be moved and getting weaker by the second.

Arkansas knew better than to argue with his friend. 'I don't like the idea of leaving you here alone,' he said 'but moving you could send that slug in further.'

'I'll be fine,' Will reiterated. 'Just leave some water in my reach and a little baccy.'

'If those rustlers come back,' Arkansas said, more thinking aloud than speaking.

'Why should they come back? They left me for dead and took everything I own.'

'Who the hell's this Lance you mentioned earlier?' Arkansas asked.

'He owns most of the land around here. He's made several offers to buy me out. Don't know why. This spread's next to worthless.'

'And you think these rustlers could be his way of running you off?'

Will shrugged his shoulders. 'Don't know,' he said. 'Maybe.'

Arkansas didn't like the sound of that one little bit. His friend's uncertainty only added to his own doubts over leaving him here while he rode into town and located the doctor. Only it had to be done and the longer they waited the less Will's chances became of surviving the current situation. If Arkansas left now he was sure he could be back well before nightfall. And he could buy some supplies; all Will had in the cabin was a little Folgers coffee, a few slices of jerky and a sorry amount of flour. He'd also be able to get some glass and repair the windows.

'I'll leave you the Spencer,' Arkansas said. 'It'll be easier to use from your position than a Colt. If anyone comes close you're not sure of, blow them to high heaven.' The Spencer required separately working the lever and pulling the hammer back, but an experienced man could let off all seven shots in a matter of seconds. Even in Will's weakened state he should have no problem with the gun.

'I'll be fine,' Will said again. 'Just leave me the water and the makings. I'll be snug and dandy. Bring some whiskey back from town with you. It'll dull the pain.'

'Doc'll have laudanum.'

'Whiskey will taste a damn sight better.'

'Sure,' Arkansas said and went outside to fill up the bucket with fresh water.

As he scooped water from the stream he suddenly had the feeling that he was being watched and he sprung erect, hands hovering above the twin Colts. But all was silent and he decided he was getting jumpy.

He made his way back to the cabin, intent on ministering to Will's wound once more, applying a fresh dressing with strips torn from a shirt he'd taken from his own saddle-bags, before leaving for the doctor.

THREE

Night was still some way off when Arkansas rode into the town of Red Rock and he didn't want to waste any time. He still had to locate the doctor and pick up some supplies. As well as food, a few ounces of Bull Durham and a bottle of whiskey, he could do with a couple of panes of glass to repair the windows back at the cabin, so he decided to get about his business immediately. He'd like to get the doc out to Will and back to town before nightfall.

He was eager to do all this without drawing too much attention to himself. If Will was right in his suspicions that the raid on his place had been a put-up job then whoever organized it could have eyes everywhere. Best to let them, whoever they were, think Will was dead, as they surely must. Red Rock was a trail town and such was the transient nature of such places, that Arkansas didn't think the sight of a stranger would be a rarity, and he felt that if he did his best to avoid drawing attention to himself then it shouldn't be too much of a problem.

He rode directly to the livery stable, dismounted and tied his horse to a rail. The stable doors were open and Arkansas walked directly inside. There was a small cart at the rear of the barn and he smiled. It would suit to take the supplies back to Will's place and he'd be able to send it back with the doc afterwards. He scanned the length of the stable but there was no one about. He was about to leave when suddenly he heard footsteps coming up behind him and, when he turned, he found himself looking down at a squat elderly man.

'You run this place?' Arkansas asked.

'I'm not standing here for the benefit of my health,' the old man said irritably. 'Names Rycot.' He offered his hand to Arkansas but the gesture was ignored. The old timer frowned.

'Where's the doc?'

'You sick?'

'Where's the doc?' Firmer, with steel.

The old man swallowed audibly. 'End of Main Street,' he said. 'Turn left into First and you'll find the doc's place on the far left, next to the newspaper offices.'

'Obliged.' Arkansas said. 'Freshen my horse up – I'll need the hire of your cart. That OK with you?'

'Sure,' the old man said, smiling a toothless, wrinkling, grin.

'Obliged,' Arkansas replied, and walked off in search of the doctor.

The doctor had taken some persuading to leave his

place and ride out into the cabin. Arkansas had told him of how he'd ridden in yesterday and found Will all shot up, perhaps even close to death. The wound was festering and the fever was on the man and bringing him to town could kill him. The argument was finally settled when Arkansas informed the doctor that either he rode out with him, or he'd been nursing his own gut wound.

Arkansas had left the man to collect his instruments and gone back to the livery stable. On the way he passed a few men in the street but he ignored them and kept his pace with grim determination.

'I've done what you asked, mister,' Rycot told him, as he saw Arkansas approach. He pointed to the cart, to which he had already rigged up a powerful-looking pack horse. The sorrel was tethered behind it. Both horses looked fresh, brushed down and watered.

'Good,' Arkansas said and reached into his jacket. He pulled out a roll of bills and counted off several. 'That should cover it,' he said, and stuffed the notes into the old man's out-stretched hand.

'Much obliged.' The old man's eyes were wide. It was twice the usual fee, but he stuffed it into his pocket all the same.

'I'll return the cart and horse later,' Arkansas said. 'Maybe even tomorrow.'

'Sure,' the old man replied. 'Where you heading?'

Arkansas gave the old man one of those looks that suggested in no uncertain terms that he stop asking fool questions.

'I'm going over to the general store,' Arkansas said,

presently. 'I'll need you to tag along and help load the cart.'

For a moment the old man looked as if he was about to protest that this wasn't part of his duties, but then, perhaps remembering how much money he'd just been given, he nodded. 'Only too pleased to help.' He smiled again but this time the gesture failed to reach his eyes. The compensation of this was that his face didn't wrinkle quite as much.

They went directly to the store and Arkansas left the old man outside while he went in to carry out his business. He emerged ten minutes later with a harassed-looking store clerk who was struggling with a large barrel of Folgers coffee beans. Arkansas held a sack of flour and they loaded their respective goods onto the cart. The store clerk needed a hand to negotiate the barrel safely onto the cart and once that was done he quickly scuttled back inside.

Arkansas looked at Rycot. 'Come on,' he said, 'there's more waiting inside.'

Rycot shrugged his shoulders and followed Arkansas back into the store.

'You're taking enough to feed an army,' Rycot said, as he slid the last of the supplies onto the old cart. He took a quick look at the back axle, knowing that it had needed attention for some time, but he guessed it would hold out for this trip. Least he hoped it would. He tested that the panes of glass Arkansas had purchased were secure besides the flour sacks.

Arkansas smiled and removed the makings from his shirt and lit himself a quirly. He handed the leather tobacco pouch to the old man while he brought a sulphur match to his smoke.

'Obliged,' the old man muttered and set about making himself a smoke that was just that little thicker than usual. He figured he'd deserved it with all this lugging and carrying.

'Looks like we got company,' Arkansas commented and watched as two men approached them from the far end of the street. Both men wore their rigs tied down and looked as if sudden violence was in their nature. There were a few people on the streets and they all gave the two men a wide berth as they passed.

'They work for John Lance,' Rycot told him and handed the tobacco back. 'They won't mean no harm. Just being nosy is all. We don't get that many strangers around these parts. Least not those buying supplies like they were planning on staying.'

Arkansas felt himself tense at the mention of the name, Lance. He stood perfectly motionless, the quirly dangling between his lips, as he watched the men approach.

'Howdy,' the taller of the two men said, as soon as they were within ten feet of Arkansas and the old man. 'Don't see too many strangers around these parts.'

'You got anything against strangers?' Arkansas asked and was aware of Rycot timidly slipping behind the cart.

'No,' the man replied, as his companion went over to the cart and took a look over the sides. 'Just being neighbourly is all.'

'Well, neighbour,' Arkansas said, 'I'd appreciate it if

your friend got away from my cart.' He allowed slight movement in his hands, ready to draw at the slightest provocation. He was hoping the threat would be enough to prevent the necessity of actually doing so.

'Clay,' the man said to his companion, 'quit rooting about in the man's property.'

The man called Clay gave his companion a puzzled look and then he directed his eyes at Arkansas. For a second it seemed as if he was going to make a play, but he seemed to decide against it and walked back over to his friend. The men exchanged glances.

'Hell,' the other man continued, 'let's not step off on the wrong foot. This here's Clay Tanner and I'm called Jim. I ain't got no more name than that since I was an orphan and no one took the time to give me no second one.'

Arkansas nodded and was aware of Rycot emerging from behind the cart. He relaxed slightly, feeling some of the tension ease between himself and the men.

'You got a name then, stranger?' Jim asked.

'Smith.' Arkansas dropped the quirly and ground it out beneath his heel. He climbed up onto the cart and took the reins in his hand. 'Arkansas Smith.'

The two men looked at each other but said nothing. The name seemed to have registered with them, as Arkansas knew it would, but neither of them made any further move. They stood there, both perfectly silent as they watched the man atop the cart.

Arkansas reached out a hand and helped the old man up and then, ignoring the two men, drove in the direction of the doctor's place.

'You really Arkansas Smith?' Rycot asked, as they turned the cart onto First Street. 'I knew you was someone. Yep, you can tell that from the way you hold yourself. Mighty proud, like a strutting rooster.'

'You calling me a chicken?'

For a moment the ostler looked unsure of himself, scared even, but then deciding Arkansas was joshing on him he smiled. 'Don't think I'd call the great Arkansas Smith a chicken, or anything else for that matter.'

Arkansas looked at him, said nothing, and merely offered a grim smile in reply. He cast a glance over his shoulder and noticed the two men called Clay and Jim had not moved and were still standing in the street. He guessed they'd try and put a bullet in his back if they could only be sure of killing him.

'I heard of you,' Rycot said. 'Everyone's heard of you. They say you were born on a battlefield. They say you're faster than all other men rolled into one. They say you once faced off six men all on your lonesome and put three of them down before they'd even cleared leather. They say you're so fast the wind can't even catch you from a standstill.' The old man became particularly animated and he slapped his thigh in delight.

'Is that what they say?' Arkansas considered Rycot with some amusement.

'Sure do.' Rycot was on a roll. 'Anything I can do to help you, Mister Smith, you just say.'

Arkansas pulled the cart to a stop outside the

doctor's whitewashed fence. 'Well, go and tell the doc I'm ready to leave,' he said. 'And I'll leave you to it.'

'Yes, sir.' Rycot gave an exaggerated salute. He hopped down from the cart with the dexterity of a man half his age. This story would be worth quite a few drinks over at the Majestic.

FOUR

Night had finally vanquished the remnants of the day.

It was a clear sky, a full moon gave the landscape an eerie glow and the cloudless heavens were studded with innumerable stars. Given the time of the year, Arkansas guessed that it was somewhere around ten o'clock. He had expected the doctor to be finished by now, but the man had not emerged from the small room where he had tended to the wounded man for more than a hour.

The slug had been removed. Arkansas had been there, assisting that part of the operation. The doc hadn't been too concerned at removing the bullet. All that was needed was a shallow incision and a deft hand with the forceps to get the slug out. Cleaning the wound presented the biggest difficulty and the doc had swabbed it several times before closing it with thick stitching. Finally, he dressed it with a field bandage, which he soaked in iodine.

'I think he'll make it,' the doctor had said, and then chased Arkansas out of the room while he set about making the patient more comfortable.

Arkansas sat on the step outside the cabin, content to wait for the doctor. He smoked and thought he'd make a start on fixing the place up come dawn. He'd repair the cabin first, fit the new glass he'd picked up in town and then he'd put the corral back together. When it became opportune he'd ride out and see if he couldn't scrape up a few mavericks and get Will back on his feet again. But that would have to wait. He didn't intend leaving his friend alone any more than was strictly necessary. The two men in town had spooked him somewhat and left an uneasy feeling. He felt as if he was missing something but was not at all sure what. There had been something about the two men that he had overlooked. Something important.

He was, however, sure of one thing: his friend's mishap had been more than a case of him having disturbed rustlers. Earlier, Will had mentioned the name Lance and then old man Rycot had said the two men in town had worked for John Lance. Arkansas wasn't sure of the exact relevance of that, or who this John Lance was, but there'd be plenty of time to find out. As soon as Will was stronger he'd question him on the subject and if it did turn out that this Lance was trying to drive Will away for whatever reason, then things would get mighty unpleasant. Arkansas intended to see to that personally.

He flicked his smoke away and watched it hit the ground, bursting into a glitter of sparks before blinking away into nothing. He was about to go back inside when the doctor came out onto the steps. His sleeves were rolled up and he was wiping his hands with a piece of cloth.

'How is he?' Arkansas asked.

The doctor gave a slight smile. 'Chances are he'll live.'

'He will,' Arkansas said firmly, as if his words carried more weight than the medic's opinion. 'Will's a tough old bird.'

'He's a very sick man,' the doctor told him and, with a groan, sat down on the step next to Arkansas. 'The bullet wasn't in too deeply, as you know, but he lay there for at least two days before you found him. It's a miracle the blood loss didn't kill him.'

'Like I said, he's a tough old bird.'

'Infection's tougher.'

Arkansas stared at the doctor with a grim expression on his face. 'He'll get through it.'

'Keep him clean, comfortable and make sure he takes plenty of fluids and I believe he may.' The doctor took a silver tin from his pocket and flipped the lid. It contained several cigars and he placed one between his teeth and stuck a match to it. He pocketed the tin without offering it to Arkansas. 'Any idea what happened?'

Arkansas shook his head. 'Maybe rustlers,' he said, and then asked, bluntly, 'Who is John Lance?'

'He's a rancher,' the doctor told him. 'The biggest and richest around these parts. This spread and only one or two others are maybe the only land around that doesn't belong to John Lance.'

'Do you know him personally?'

'I've ministered him in the past,' the doctor said. 'And his daughter, but I don't really know that much about him. John Lance has an office in town but he pretty much keeps himself to himself. No one really knows him, only by sight. He seems a tough old bird.'

Silence fell between the two men and lasted for some time, both of them lost in their own private thoughts. It was the doctor who finally spoke.

'Why do you ask about John Lance?'

'No reason.' Arkansas gave the doctor a look that ensured the subject was dropped there and then.

'I think I'll wait until first light before heading back to town,' the doctor told him. 'I can check on the patient again in the morning. Change the dressing and such before I get on my way.'

'Sure,' Arkansas said. 'Sorry it ain't more comfortable around here but I plan on getting this place fixed up as soon as I can.'

'Coffee'd be good right about now,' the doctor said and tossed the remains of his cigar into the night.

'I've got some on the stove.'

'I know,' the doctor said. 'It's sure giving off a delicious aroma.'

Arkansas stood and was about to go back into the cabin when he suddenly froze. He held up a hand to silence the doctor and peered out into the night. There was someone out there: he had heard the unmistakable sound of a human whisper.

'What's the matter?'

Arkansas looked at the doctor and held a finger to his lips. He continued to stare out into the night. He had definitely heard it and it had been the sound of a man. Of that there was no doubt – true it had been nothing more than a faint whisper, but Arkansas knew a man when he heard one.

'Inside. Quickly.'

He followed the doctor inside and then drew his Colt. 'There's someone out there,' he said. 'Someone who doesn't want to be seen.'

'Are you sure?'

Arkansas nodded and went back to the open doorway. He stood there, gazing out into the darkness, his Colt hanging limply by his side. Someone was watching them and it was further confirmation, if more were needed, that the attack on Will had been more than a case of simply disturbing rustlers. Whoever was responsible they were out there now, watching the place. Arkansas had no idea what they had in mind, but whatever it was he would be ready for them.

'What're you going to do?' thie doctor asked.

'Nothing I can do,' Arkansas replied. 'Other than wait.'

'All night?'

'If I have to.' He turned to look at the doctor and then shrugged his shoulders. And then suddenly he swung back around and looked out into the night. He could hear someone moving about, no, not someone, more than one. It sounded like two people and they seemed to be going away. This was confirmed when, moments later, Arkansas heard the faint sound of two horses being spurred into movement.

'What's the matter?' the doctor asked, sensing Arkansas's mood.

'Whoever it was, they're gone.'

Arkansas had the feeling that whoever had been out there, had something to do with the two men he had seen in town earlier. It might have even been them, the men who had called themselves Clay and Jim. The way he figured it they had been curious, and probably had good reason for that curiosity. And they had followed a good ways behind when he'd left town with the doc. If they had been responsible for what had happened to Will, then they must have assumed they'd left him for dead.

Until now that is. Now, they would know that he was very much alive, and that kind of knowledge could provoke some sort of action.

Arkansas crossed the room and took a bottle of whiskey from the table. He unscrewed the cap and drank directly from the bottle. He suddenly felt very tired and he figured he'd chance a few hours' sleep.

'Help yourself to that coffee,' Arkansas offered.

The doctor nodded. 'Right now, he said, 'I'd sooner have a little of that whiskey.'

Arkansas handed the bottle to the doctor and without further words, bedded down on the floor next to the door. Within seconds he seemed to be in a deep sleep. It was a skill Arkansas had picked up in the years sleeping beneath the stars, when sudden danger was potentially never more than a split second away. In such circumstances a man had to snatch whatever rest he could. You never knew when the next opportunity would come along.

The doctor took a slug from the bottle and then went over to the most comfortable-looking chair. He sat down and drank some more and then stared at the sleeping figure on the floor.

There was no doubt about it, this Arkansas Smith was a curious man. A most curious man indeed.

Ah, well, he thought and took another mouthful of the whiskey.

'That guy's going to be trouble,' Jim said, and steadied his horse. He sent it forward slowly across the stream. 'He's got a reputation and if he's pally with McCord then we could be looking at trouble.'

'You don't think McCord's dead?'

Jim shook his head. Clay could be mighty stupid at times. 'With that Arkansas fellow there and the doctor – what do you think?'

Clay considered carefully for the moment and then, seeming to agree it made sense, asked, 'So what do we do?'

'We go tell the boss.' Jim said, and spurred his horse into a gallop. His companion followed and together they galloped off into the night.

YESTERYEAR

'Savages.' Walter Smith spat and took a look at the carnage around him.

He felt for his rifle on the floor and, with a smile to his wife, placed it on the wagon seat beside them. He could see the concern in Edith's face and he placed an arm around her shoulder, pulling her tighter to him. 'They're long gone. We're in no danger.'

'It's terrible,' Edith said. 'Why do they do this?'

'Don't look.' The old man jumped down from the wagon. He gave his wife one of his handguns and took the rifle with him. 'Just to be on the safe side.'

'What are you doing?' Edith asked, fear very much evident in her voice. She was visibly upset, which was to be expected since they had just come across a body-strewn battlefield. Not something a woman should see. Not something anyone should see. 'Come back here.'

'I have to take a look around,' the old man told her with a frown. 'I won't be far. Anything happens you holler and I'll come running.'

Before Edith could protest further her husband started off across the field, stepping around hideously mutilated bodies. There were several burnt-out wagons scattered around, a few of them were still smouldering, and the smell of smoke and burning flesh hung heavy in the air. There was such an atmosphere that it seemed as if the screams of the dead could still be heard in the air as ghostly echoes of what had happened here.

Walter shuddered and held the rifle tightly to his chest. At his feet there was a dead girl, a child really, no more than ten or eleven. Her head had been split down the middle by a heavy axe. The gory gash had parted her head and her eyes were so many inches apart they could have belonged to two different people.

He said a silent prayer and stepped over her.

Everywhere he looked there were dead bodies, many of them with arrows protruding from their bodies, some mutilated, scalped, others with no obvious wounds. Many of them were naked and a good number of them had been burnt, charred clothing sticking to blackened flesh. Ahead of him there was a pile of bodies, maybe ten to twelve people, all stacked up one atop the other. Into this gruesome heap the Indians had shot arrow after arrow and then set it alight only the flames hadn't taken and it was a ghastly sight. It looked like some bizarre human totem pole.

Other than the gentle flapping of the canvas on his wagon behind him, there was nothing to be heard and, standing there Walter felt a chill run the length of his spine. The place became eerie in its silence and he decided to get out of here and report this at the nearest army post.

Didn't look like he could do anything for these folks, in any case. The only one who could help them now was the

Almighty himself. And it seemed as if he had forsaken this place, relinquished the land rights to the Devil. He looked up into a clear sky and saw several buzzards circling, waiting for him to move on so they could claim the flesh that now belonged to them.

'I'm coming, Edith.' He turned and waved to his wife on the wagon. Though she had said nothing and simply sat on the wagon, her face visibly sickened even from Walt's position.

It gave him the creeps and he tasted bile in the back of his throat.

He started back to the wagon, carefully picking his footing so as not to step on any of the dead when he suddenly heard a movement and froze. He lifted his rifle and turned from side to side where he stood, searching for the source of the sound. But a perfect silence greeted him.

You're getting easily spooked, he told himself. Must be getting old, too soft for this life. But there it was again, a faint sound and he stood perfectly still, listening. It was a whimper and he realized his wife had heard it too. She was standing up in the wagon and pointing over to a burnt-out wagon, the skeletal frame looking so fragile that it would blow to dust if the wind picked up some.

Walt started to walk quicker towards the remains of the wagon and, when he got there, the sight that greeted him almost stopped his heart. He was a big man and had seen much cruelty in his time but this was like nothing he had ever experienced and he felt a shudder run through him.

'Woman,' he shouted to his wife, 'get over here. Bring a blanket and that whiskey I keep under the seat.'

He stood there, silently, while he waited.

There on the ground was a woman; she looked unmarked,

35

but was most definitely dead. Between her legs, naked on the ground, was a baby. It was still attached to her by the umbilical cord, but where the mother had departed this world the baby, a boy, was alive but only just. She couldn't have given birth too long ago and when Walt knelt and touched her she was still slightly warm, but there was no pulse, no heartbeat. The woman stared back at him with empty eyes and he closed the lids with fingers. Left weakened and with no one to tend to her, she must have died giving birth. The baby though, by some miracle, had made it thus far: there was at least one survivor of the massacre.

'My dear God,' Edith said, standing next to her husband. She held a thick blanket and the half-drunk bottle of whiskey. She smiled weakly at her husband. 'The poor little thing.'

Walt took the whiskey from her, mouthed a long slug and then pulled his Bowie from his waistband. He poured some of the whiskey over the blade, catching the drips under his free hand. He then licked the sodden hand and knelt and held the umbilical cord in one hand and took his knife to it, slicing it clean, close to the baby's body. There was a quick spurt of blood and the child let out a weak and pathetic cry.

The old man picked up the baby and handed it to his wife and the warmth of the blanket.

The poor mite felt spindly and weak.

'Born on a battlefield,' Walt said.

Had a child ever had a worse start to life?

Edith's eyes filled with tears. She held the baby close to her, warming its clammy skin. They both knew the child had virtually no chance of survival but they had to try. They had the house cow tethered to the wagon which would provide milk, so at the very least they could feed the poor thing, so there was a slim chance that they could save the child.

'Arkansas,' Walt said. 'Call him Arkansas. Since that's where we is.'

'Arkansas Smith.' Edith said and smiled when the baby gripped one of her fingers in a tiny fist. He seemed to approve of the name. 'I think he likes it. '

In truth, they had yet to cross the Missouri border and Arkansas was still some miles off. The old man had never been the best of navigators and by the time they reached Fort Comanche and learnt their mistake the name had come to suit the baby. Arkansas it would remain. Good job I didn't think we were in Dung City, the old man had often joked.

FIVE

With the advent of first light the doctor again changed Will's dressing, paying particular attention to the pus and gore on the spent one. There was some infection, but he said he expected Will would be able to fight through it. He placed a thick poultice beneath the fresh dressing and then nodded with satisfaction. He would call at the cabin every other day for at least a week, he promised, and then gave Arkansas strict instructions as to his friend's care. Fluids, and not of the rye-based kind, were important. Water, some coffee was permissible. And it was imperative that Will eat a little several times a day if he was to regain the strength to fight the sapping fever that had set in. He had left a bottle of medicine for the pain and said he would apply a fresh poultice to the wound the next visit.

The doctor had then left for town.

Arkansas had offered to escort him, but the medic insisted on going alone, he would have no trouble handling the horse and cart and besides, the doc had

38

pointed out, Arkansas's talents were better suited here, in care of his friend. Arkansas had to admit the doctor had a good point there. And although the doctor didn't say anything it was evident from his manner that he was eager to go. Perhaps he was spooked at Arkansas's suggestion that someone had been watching the cabin overnight. After all, it was an irrefutable fact that Will had been attacked and shot in this very cabin. Someone had sure enough done that.

Arkansas had watched the doctor ride out of sight and then immediately set about fixing up the cabin. He had checked on Will but found his friend in a deep, drug-induced sleep, his breathing sounding regular and strong as his body fought off the infection that was currently seeping poison through his body.

He was going to make it: Arkansas was sure of it. He closed the bedroom door and set about righting the damage done to the place. The windows took a while to fix; the panes of glass Arkansas had bought in town slotted in perfectly to their frames, but Arkansas had to use small nails to secure the glass in place. Once that was done he started on the fence and after several hours of backbreaking but enjoyable work he had the corral together.

He stood back, wiped sweat from his brow, and admired the results of his toil. The place looked as good as new and it would take a very sharp eye to find any sign of the destruction that had happened here only days ago.

Arkansas went back inside to check on Will. He

found him awake, sitting up in bed. His complexion looked better now that his usual colour had returned to his cheeks, but there was a thin sheen of sweat on his forehead and his grey hair looked slick. His eyes were clear with no sign of the bloodshot so evident only this morning.

'How you feeling?'

Will gave a weak smile. 'Like I was stampeded on by a herd of buffalo and then some.'

'That good?' Arkansas said with a smile, and poured a cup of water from the pitcher on the upturned crate. He handed it to Will who now had the strength to take the glass and guide it to his own lips.

'Thanks,' Will said, after draining the entire cup. 'I must be on the mend,' he said. 'I'm starving. I could eat a horse.'

'I could fix some eggs and bacon,' Arkansas said. 'I picked up some supplies in town when I got the doc.'

'Sounds good,' Will said, and winced at a sudden wave of pain. 'My side feels like it's been kicked by a mule.'

'A forty-four calibre mule,' Arkansas replied, and was about to go and prepare the meal when he heard a scream from outside.

A woman's scream, shrill, panicked, terrified.

Arkansas grabbed the Spencer and handed it to Will and then, his own Colt clear of leather, he ran outside.

'You said he was dead.' John Lance paced the small room, a cigar clamped between his teeth. 'You said

40

you'd killed him. And yet now you come here and tell me this?' Small specks of ash fell from the cigar as he spoke. 'Kill you two is what I should do.'

Clay and Jim exchanged looks and then glanced towards Jake for assistance, but none was forthcoming. Jake, ranch foreman of the Double L, right-hand man to John Lance, and good friend of both Jim and Clay, stood there at the door and looked on impassively. If he was going to speak up for them he was taking his time about it.

'Tell me about this Arkansas Smith,' Lance said, and flicked the ash from his cigar.

For a moment there was silence as both Jim and Clay fidgeted, neither of them wanting to take the initiative.

'Well?'

It was Jim who spoke. 'That's who he said he was. I don't know if he is, or where he came from, or how he got here. All we know is that he took the doc out to McCord's place.'

The two men had ridden through the night and then spent the best part of the morning debating whether to tell Lance about the doctor and the newcomer who claimed to be Arkansas Smith. In the end they decided it was prudent to do so. They didn't tell him though that they had doubled back and confronted Dr Cooter on the way back to town. The way things were going they decided to keep that to themselves.

'You evidently didn't kill McCord.' Lance didn't like this turn of events at all. If McCord had survived,

41

which seemed likely, and named Jim and Clay as the men that had attacked him, then that would implicate his own good name. They worked for him and maybe the law would see that they had been acting on his orders when they had shot him. And what of this Arkansas Smith? This man with a big reputation? 'I should kill you two,' he snarled again, as if there was no other option.

'Weren't our fault, sir,' Clay said. 'I shot McCord myself.'

'Then you'd do better to leave the whiskey alone and improve your aim,' Lance told him and tossed the stub of his cigar into the fireplace. 'You two'll have to hide out somewhere until we know what's happening. If McCord names you two you'd be better off away from here. We'd all be better off.'

'I don't think he'd know we was behind it,' Jim said, 'even if he does survive.'

'No?' Lance looked out of the window, the sky brilliantly blue, and the sun impossibly bright.

'No,' Jim shook his head. 'We and the other boys went in too quickly. Clay plugged McCord as soon as he appeared in the bedroom doorway. It happened too fast for him to have seen anything.'

'And he weren't moving when we ransacked the place,' Clay added. 'He sure looked dead to me.'

'That's too much chance for me to take. Not now that we're so close,' Lance said. 'No, until we find out what's going on, I want you two far away from here. I'll send word when I want you to return.'

Jim and Clay looked at each other and then to Jake

42

for support, but, once again, none was forthcoming. Lance continued to pace the room, seemingly lost in thought. A long silence hung over the room until John Lance turned on his feet and took a long lingering look at the two cowboys.

'The fact that McCord may be alive doesn't change anything. We've got the signed document.'

Both men nodded, eagerly. The document was the important thing. At least that part of their mission had been a success.

'Clear out immediately,' Lance said, and pinched the bridge of his nose against the startings of a headache. 'Ride over to the old Bowen place. Hide out there and stay put until you hear otherwise.' His voice was firm and everyone in that room knew there was no point offering further argument.

John Lance had spoken.

SIX

If he'd had time to consider the situation Arkansas might have found the sight that greeted him amusing. As it was there was no such time and he ran to his horse, which he had always kept saddled, and spurred her into an immediate gallop.

The object of his pursuit – a woman, who had come from God alone knew where – was holding on for dear life and screaming as her horse, a pure white creature, galloped. It reached the corral fence and then veered off to the left, caused the woman to slip in her saddle and she screamed even louder as she felt her grip on the reins loosening. Any moment now and it seemed she'd be thrown to the hard ground.

Arkansas spurred his horse harder, gaining more speed from the sorrel that had suited him so well in so many tricky situations and, true to form, she gave him the extra push needed to gain on the other horse. Arkansas reached out and grabbed the reins of the woman's horse and then by pulling his own sorrel back, he expertly brought it to a halt. He dismounted and then held out his arms, helping the woman down.

'Snake,' she said, unsteady on her feet so that Arkansas had to support her.

'There's no need to call me that,' Arkansas said, amused.

'Spooked my horse.' Her eyes suddenly rolled backwards and she fainted away into Arkansas' arms.

He smiled. Typical, he thought. He'd never seen a woman who didn't faint clean away after a spell of blood-rushing excitement. He lifted her into his arms and carried her back to the cabin where he intended to revive her with a little water.

She was a beautiful woman. Her skin was handsomely tanned, almost coffee coloured. She had a round face with thick red lips and luxurious black hair that fell down over her slender shoulders. Her eyes, currently closed, had been a chocolate brown. Arkansas would have placed her age somewhere around the mid twenties.

He placed her down gently on the floor, since there was nowhere else suitable and Will had the one and only bed. And then went and dipped his bandanna in a bucket of water. He swabbed at the side of her neck, all the while resting her head in his hand. She stirred gently and then her eyes snapped open and she sat up.

'What happened?' she asked.

Arkansas stood back up. He put the bandanna down on an upturned crate. 'Your horse bolted,' he said. 'You said something about a snake.'

'Yes,' she said, and Arkansas noticed that her eyes were as warm and inviting as a summer's day. 'It seems we ran for miles. Is my horse OK?'

'Will be,' Arkansas said. 'I tethered it out back. It's drinking a lake of water at the moment. Just needs a little rest is all.'

'Thank you,' she said. 'Mister, er—?'

'Smith,' Arkansas said. 'Arkansas Smith.' This time the name didn't seem to get any special reaction.

She smiled and the gesture seemed to set off a celestial display within her eyes. 'Thank you,' she repeated. 'I've Rebecca La—' Her words were cut off by a yell of enquiry from Will in the other room; he wanted to know, in his own words, what the hell-fire and brimstone was going on.

'It's OK, Will,' Arkansas shouted. 'Just a young lady out riding and lost control of her horse.' He shrugged his shoulders and went through to the other room. The woman followed behind.

'Is he all right?' Rebecca asked.

'Sure,' Arkansas took the Spencer from Will and rested it against the wall. 'Will's been shot but it's not the first time.'

'Probably won't be that last,' Will said, and laughed but then groaned and held his side as a fresh wave of pain reminded him all too clearly of his situation. Rebecca went to him and held one of his hands tightly. 'I nursed during the war,' she said. 'You must let me help.'

'Ain't nothing but a flesh wound,' Will protested.

'You must let me help,' Rebecca insisted.

Arkansas shrugged his shoulders. 'Sure,' he said. 'But don't you have somewhere you have to go?'

'No.'

'Kin who'll be wondering where you are?' Arkansas frowned at the woman. She was well dressed and obviously a woman of some means. She had to have come from somewhere.

Rebecca's face clouded over momentarily. 'Only Daddy,' she said. 'But he won't notice. He won't be home for hours yet.'

'Well,' Arkansas said, rubbing the back of his head, 'there's nothing really for you to do. He's seen a doctor. Just needs rest is all.'

'Nonsense,' Rebecca said. 'There's plenty I could do. I can give this place a proper clean up for a start. And I could cook you two something before I leave.' She smiled, warmly. 'I'd like to thank you for saving me and my horse.'

'That would be dandy,' Will said. 'I think I could manage a little food made proper and all.'

'Shoot,' Arkansas said. For some reason that he couldn't understand he was feeling awkward in the company of the woman. He rolled his eyes and went outside for a smoke.

'I don't rightly know, Sheriff,' John Lance said, and sucked on one of his large Juan de Fuca cigars. 'All I do know is that this Arkansas Smith, a known gunfighter, is out there. McCord being dead or alive is beyond my knowledge since no one can find the town doctor to ask him just what his business was out there.'

'Doc does this from time to time,' Sheriff Bill Hackman said and sat back in his chair, resting his hands on his ample belly. 'He'll be off drunk and most likely with some whore. He'll turn up when he's good and ready. And there are no papers that I know of on any Arkansas Smith. I looked through everything we have and as far as I can tell he ain't wanted for anything anywhere.'

Lance frowned. 'So exactly what do you know of this Arkansas character?'

'Only what folk say,' the sheriff replied. 'That's he's fast with a gun. Maybe the fastest.'

'You're sheriff,' Lance said. 'You should know what goes on around here. The doctor rode out to the McCord place with a stranger and you knew nothing about it.'

'I can't be expected to see every move anyone ever makes,' Hackman protested. 'I'm the only law in this town and I'm often dealing with a million things at the same time.'

'You seemed busy enough when we rode in.' Lance's words dripped heavy with sarcasm. They had arrived an hour ago and found the sheriff slumbering behind his desk.

'I was resting my eyes. Ain't had much time to sleep lately.' The sheriff ran his hands through his hair. 'I'm run ragged these days.'

Lance leaned over the desk, his knuckles white against the rich wood, and blew cigar smoke over the sheriff.

'I'm intending to take possession of the McCord property on the first of the month, as is my legal right, and I expect you to ensure that legal right is not

48

impeded in any way.' His eyes blazed with a thunderous threat and the sheriff sat upright. 'That's in four days' time,' Lance concluded, and went over to the window and looked out onto the street.

'Of course.' Hackman said. 'I'm the law and I will see the law done.'

'You are the law.' Lance nodded but didn't look away from the window and added, 'My law. Don't forget that.'

The sheriff nodded. 'Yes, sir. I know who calls the shots in this town. Don't you think I already know that?' Defeated, he skulked off into the back of the building to where he kept his whiskey.

SEVEN

The following morning Arkansas woke a little later than was usual. He put this down to the substantial meal the woman Rebecca had prepared before leaving the previous evening. Even Will had managed half a bowl of the delicious stew and had then fallen into a contented sleep. Arkansas's care had been all very well, but there was something about a woman's touch when it came to getting chow done.

Arkansas stood on the porch, smoking a quirly, drinking a tin cup of strong coffee and looked off at the far horizon. He had to give Will credit, it was a beautiful land. If someone was looking to settle down this was as good a place as any. In the distance, snow-capped mountains could be seen, Ponderosa pines reaching towards the sky.

Later, after tending to Will who was looking better than ever and now able to sit up in bed, Arkansas took the sorrel out for a quick look around. He didn't want to go too far from the cabin until he knew for certain who had done for his friend. Before leaving, he had armed Will with the Spencer. You could never be too

50

careful; they had both learned that valuable lesson long ago, and the rifle's .54-calibre slug provided ample insurance against further unwanted visitors.

Arkansas kept the cabin in sight and merely circled the perimeter around the building. He could see why Will had picked this spot to lay his land claim. The valley was protected from all sides by densely planted mountains and a stream ran down from those hills and went directly through Will's land. Water could often be a valuable commodity in long summers when the rain refused to come. He was about to go further into the mountain when he saw three men riding towards him.

He turned the sorrel and spurred it into a gallop back towards the cabin. He wasn't sure who the mounted men were but he wanted to be close to his friend if it meant further trouble.

He reached the cabin and sent the sorrel into the corral.

He ran into the cabin and went through to Will. 'Someone's coming.'

Will sat up in bed, wincing slightly with the effort. He grabbed the Spencer from beside the bed where he'd left it. 'How many?'

'Three men.'

'What do you think?'

Arkansas shrugged his shoulders. He supposed they could be anyone – drifters, men in search of work. But then again, by the same token they could be connected with whoever it was had attacked Will in the first place.

'Be ready with that Spencer,' Arkansas said. 'I'll go

out and meet them.'

'Be careful.'

Arkansas smiled, grimly. 'As always.'

Arkansas got back outside just as the three men reached the corral fence. He stood in the doorway, watching them.

'Looks empty,' a well-dressed man said. He was obviously the leader of this particular trio. The other men held their horses level with him, one each side.

'State your business,' Arkansas said.

The man who had spoken earlier smiled. 'I'm John Lance,' he said. 'I'm here to speak with William McCord.'

Arkansas took a long lingering look at Lance before speaking. He was bigger than he'd imagined him to be and looked oversized on his horse. 'About what?'

'My business is with McCord,' Lance said. 'You have me at a disadvantage. Who might you be?'

Arkansas smiled. 'That depends.'

Suddenly the atmosphere between them became charged and the men either side of John Lance tensed, readying themselves for action should the need arise.

'Depends on what?' John Lance asked.

'On you starting trouble,' Arkansas told him. 'Then you'll find out who I am. Then you'll find out quick and good.'

The two riders suddenly became alert at the implied threat, but John Lance held up a hand to steady his men. He shifted in his saddle, trying not to show how the over confident man was making him feel.

'May I speak with McCord?' Lance asked.

'No,' Arkansas said. 'You may not.' He stared at the men with Lance and locked eyes with each of them in turn, willing them to make a play.

'And may I ask why?'

Arkansas smiled at Lance. 'Because he's recuperating,' he said, 'after being shot by some low down skunk. But he'll be fine on account of that skunk's a poor shot.'

'Oh dear,' John Lance said. 'That is most unfortunate and I sympathize. But I'm here to iron out details of taking possession of this place.'

'Possession?' Arkansas was confused.

'Why yes,' John Lance said. 'I bought this place from Mr McCord.'

Arkansas hadn't expected this. It made no sense. Surely Will would have said if he'd sold the place to Lance. Even in his present state he surely would have mentioned that little fact. He'd said the man had made several offers to buy him out, but he hadn't said he'd taken him up on the deal.

What was Lance trying to pull here?

'Can you prove that?' Arkansas asked.

'Of course. The documentation's in town, lodged with both my lawyer and the sheriff. As of the first of the month this place becomes mine. I'm afraid I'll have to insist that you and McCord vacate the premises. 'Course as a gesture of goodwill I'm more than willing to arrange a bed at my hotel for McCord to recuperate from his injury.'

It suddenly came to Arkansas. The thing that had

been bothering him about the two men he had seen in town when collecting the doc, the men who had worked for Lance. One of them had been wearing a fancy-looking gun, the handle of which was identical to the knife he'd found in the cabin. He'd thought it had looked familiar because it had been Will's. Yet he'd seen the same ornate pattern on the cowboy but its significance hadn't registered until now.

'I saw two of your men in town the other day,' Arkansas said. 'Two stupid-looking brutes.' He cast his eyes at the men either side of Lance. 'Just as stupid-looking as these men.'

Both men flinched at the insult and made a move to their guns, but before either of them could reach their weapon, Arkansas's Colt had cleared leather. No one had really seen him move. It was as if the gun had just appeared there in his hand.

'I wouldn't,' Arkansas told them. 'Now, ride away, John Lance, and take your lies with you.'

Lance's face clouded over and thunder entered his eyes. 'I'll be back in three days, Arkansas Smith.' He smiled and then spat onto the ground. 'Oh, I know who you are. I'll be back and I'll have the law with me.'

'Sure,' Arkansas said, feeling he'd like nothing better than to put a bullet between John Lance's eyes here and now. The temptation to do so and damn the consequences was great. Only these days he didn't do things that way. 'Watch out for rustlers as you go,' he said with a grim smile.

John Lance looked at Arkansas for a moment and

then made the sign of the cross and again spat onto the ground.

He turned his horse and spurred it forward. His men followed close behind.

Arkansas stood watching them until they were out of sight and then went back inside and retrieved the knife from the crate. He held it up in view of his friend.

'Is this yours?' he asked. Will shook his head, confused. 'What was all that about out there?'

Arkansas turned the knife over and over in his hand. He looked at his friend and then smiled. 'This,' he said, enigmatically, 'proves that the men who shot you were working for John Lance.'

'What do you mean?' Will asked, his face a blueprint for confusion.

'We need to talk.' Arkansas sat on the edge of the bed, tossed the knife down on the bedspread and told his friend of the events of moments ago.

'The two-bit, fork-tongued skunk,' Will said, after listening to Arkansas's story. 'I never sold him anything. I'd burn this place before I'd sell to that no good varmint.'

'Which is what I thought,' Arkansas said. 'He say's he's got the legal papers.'

Will frowned. 'Papers?'

'Forgeries no doubt.' Arkansas placed the knife into his waistband and stood up from the bed. He crossed the room and then lingered in the doorway for a moment before turning back to his friend. 'John Lance is going to wish he had never been born.'

YESTERYEAR

Arkansas Smith, ten years old, finding himself the man of the house, stood at the graveside long after the other mourners had departed. He stared into the open ground, aware of two men waiting impatiently to fill it in, to pack the soil on top of the cheap coffin for all eternity. But he ignored them and was unable to move.

As soon as he walked away and the grave was filled in it would be final. Walter Smith would be no more.

He didn't want to take that step; as if staying here, refusing to move, would somehow delay the moment when the old man's death became a part of history. He wasn't really his father, no blood relation, but the man he thought of as his father anyway. The man who had found him as a newborn, still attached to his dead mother, and promptly named him Arkansas because that's where they were. Only they weren't, he would later discover and tell the boy years later, but the name had stuck.

Blood kin or not, the young boy couldn't have wanted for better parents than Walter and Edith Smith and he was proud to carry their name.

'*Arkansas.*'

The shout came through the mist like a phantom and Arkansas spun on his feet and saw the woman he called his mother standing at the bottom of the hill that served as the cemetery in these parts.

She was waving to him, telling him to come down from there now. His father was dead and only the body rested in the grave. He was with the Lord now and life had to go on.

Arkansas waved back and then once more said a silent goodbye to the man. He turned and caught the stare of the two gravediggers and offered a weak smile, but they bowed their heads to the ground, understanding his grief.

He walked down the hill and met the elderly woman and together they made their way back to the small, two-roomed house at the far end of town. As small as it was, it was going to feel mighty big now with Walter Smith gone.

Winter drew in quickly that year. The summer seemed to bypass the fall and head directly to the sub zero temperatures of the Illinois winter. It was early October and for the past three days freezing rain had fallen and was now giving way to snow. As the temperature dropped further still, the wet ground hardened and ice patches formed. Travelling even the smallest distances became impossible.

Arkansas shivered as he carried the bucket of water from the well. He had found the well frozen over and had had to spend several uncomfortable moments cracking the ice with an axe, the handle of which stuck to his leather gloves. He felt snow fluttering against his face, which made a change from the stinging rain, but he took no pleasure from it.

The snowfall would only make an already hard existence

harder still.

The clement summer had been too dry and the larger part of the crops had failed. They had moved here three years ago from Georgia because Walter Smith saw farming opportunities, but when the old man died all they had been left with were debts and land that had refused to provide bounty.

'It's getting colder.' Arkansas placed the bucket in the corner. He threw another log onto the fire, recoiling from the sparks that shot out, and smiled at his mother. 'I'll go and chop some more wood later,' he said. 'Just in case the snow takes hold.'

'You're a good boy.' Edith Smith closed her eyes, enjoying the warmth as the flames flickered and danced in shadows upon her face. The wind howled around the building, shaking the walls, the sound of snow tapped the window and rattled the panes of glass.

It made the place seem all the more cosy.

They sat in silence for several moments, the only sound being the logs spitting on the fire and the wind. It sounded desolate as if the world outside had ceased to exist and they were all that remained.

'You know something?' Arkansas asked, breaking the silence and poking at the fire with a twig to spread the heat around.

'What?' Edith smiled at her son and her eyes for the briefest of moments seemed to glow with a long forgotten youth. Her skin was bright in the warm reflection of the flames.

'I think you should cook up a big old pot of your stew,' Arkansas said. 'Put some warmth in our bellies.'

'That'd be nice.'

'I can go kill a turkey,' Arkansas said. 'Won't be the same as beef but it'll go down all the same.'

She nodded. 'I've got some carrots and onions in the root cellar. I'll do it later,' she said. 'Later.' Soon she was asleep.

EIGHT

The following morning was overcast. The weather matched Arkansas's mood as he pulled the sorrel to a stop outside the livery stable and dismounted. Rycot immediately ran out to greet him, a smile on his face that was soon replaced by a worried frown.

'My cart,' Rycot said. 'I was expecting it back by now.'

Arkansas looked at the man. 'The doc didn't return them?'

'No.' Rycot shook his head.

'Have you seen him?'

'Who?'

It was Arkansas's turn to frown. 'The doc.'

'No, ain't seen him since he rode out with you. The horse came in on its own yesterday, but no cart. I thought you'd bring it in when you were good and ready.'

'Don't sound right,' Arkansas said. He thought about the men hiding in the dark. Had they still been there come daylight and attacked the doc? That didn't make any sense and he didn't have time to ponder it too much at the moment. The doctor hadn't kept to his promise of attending the cabin, but Will had said that was usual for the doc who often went off on drunken benders. Not that it mattered since Will's fever was close to breaking and he seemed stronger by the hour.

'Tend to my horse. I need to see the sheriff,' Arkansas said.

That morning Arkansas had decided that Will would be safe on his own for a few hours while Arkansas rode into town to check up on John Lance's claims, view the documents the man had claimed were lodged with the sheriff.

'So where's my cart?' Rycot asked. He seemed not to grasp the implications of the situation.

'Search me,' Arkansas said, and then more firmly, 'Take care of my horse.'

Lance turned from the window and smiled. 'That Arkansas Smith gets around.'

'He don't look so tough to me.'

Lance looked at the man known simply as Pug on account of his nose having been broken one too many times, and smiled. Pug was Lance's enforcer and he had been with him for the best part of a decade. Prior to that the big man's life was a mystery and that's the way he seemed to want to keep it. Rumours were that he had been a bandit, a killer of men, and violator of women; in short, an all-round sadistic bastard. Lance thought that was most likely.

'I reckon you could take him,' Lance said, and he really did believe that. 'Course, Arkansas had a reputation as a fast gun. He'd demonstrated that back at McCord's place, but then Pug was no slouch himself. If they could provoke some kind of fight and Pug finished Arkansas then that would make things a whole lot easier for John Lance, but if it went the other way then he would have lost a very good man.

It was a risk Lance felt worth taking.

'I suppose I could,' Pug said, in his rough nasal voice, which was also the result of his multiple fractures.

The other man in the room was Jake, the ranch foreman, and he smiled conspiratorially at Lance before addressing Pug. 'You could rip him apart limb from limb.'

Pug nodded and a look of evil crossed his face.

Lance had a thriving cattle business and his Red Rock business premises were perfectly suited to such a growing concern. Situated in the centre of Main Street, lodged between the Diamond Theatre and the First Bank, it was a spacious building where Lance would often entertain clients.

'Arkansas dead,' Lance mused, 'would save us a lot of trouble when we go to take McCord's spread.'

Pug nodded. He understood what his boss was saying.

'You'll have to provoke him into a fight,' Lance told him. 'Kill him legally, in front of witnesses. The sheriff gets a bit jumpy – I'd rather not give him anything else to worry about.'

Again Pug nodded but remained silent.

Lance watched Arkansas through the window. For a moment he thought he was coming to the offices but then he veered off and went into the telegraph place.

'He's gone in the telegraph office,' Lance said. 'I wonder why he'd want to send a telegram.'

Pug shrugged his massive shoulders. He wasn't much of a one for thinking.

'Get him when he comes out,' Lance suggested.

'I'll get him,' Pug said, his voice calm and even. 'Don't you worry none about that.'

Lance smiled weakly and watched his man go outside. He knew Pug was good with the gun, fast and usually hit what he shot at. But he couldn't help feeling that he was sending him to his grave.

Arkansas folded the receipt, placed it in his shirt pocket and paid the telegraph operator.

'You should get a reply by morning,' Arkansas said. 'I'll be back.'

'Yes, sir.' The telegraph officer, a short myopic man, who had been most impressed to notice the telegram was going to the Presidential office in Washington, peered over the top his bifocals and smiled. 'Yes indeed.'

'Obliged,' Arkansas said, and went out into the now powerful afternoon sunshine. The morning cloud had lifted and it had turned into a glorious day, though there was a faint hint of the coming winter in the air.

He had to shield his eyes against the glare and it took some moments for his eyesight to adjust after the murky interior of the small telegraph office. He looked up and down Main Street – it must have been close to noon now and the town was a hive of activity. Folk walked up and down the street, going about their business. Music escaped from the batwings of the Diamond Theatre. From across the street the dim thud of Rycot at work on his anvil could be heard, perhaps taking the frustration over his missing cart on some unfortunate piece of metal.

Arkansas shook his head. The doc's disappearance was troubling as was the seeming lack of interest. If Rycot's horse had come into town rider-less yesterday then surely the sheriff should have undertaken some sort of investigation into the doctor's whereabouts. Had Rycot even informed the sheriff? Arkansas crossed the street towards the sheriff's office. He wanted to enquire about Lance's claims to Will's place so he could kill two birds with one stone.

'What did you call me?'

Arkansas had been aware of the big man walking behind him but he had paid him no mind. At first he though the big man had been addressing someone else but then the booming voice sounded again.

'You ignoring me, mister?'

Arkansas turned and looked at the biggest, most unruly-looking man he had seen for some time. The man seemed to be close on seven feet and equally as wide. He was also as ugly as he was big.

'I think your ears are playing tricks,' Arkansas said.

'What?' The big man stood rigid, hands hanging at his side, the classic gunfighter pose.

64

'There you are,' Arkansas said, with a smile. 'They're doing it again.' He made to walk off, but then the big man spoke again and this time his words held much more menace. He sounded primed to explode.

'Don't turn away, coward. Turn and face me.'

Arkansas did so. 'You don't want to do this.'

The big man grinned. 'You insulted me, stranger. I don't take that from no man.'

'I insulted no one,' Arkansas said firmly. 'Though, now you come to mention it, you are one stupid-looking, ugly son-of-a-bitch.'

The large man went beserk, which was what Arkansas was hoping for. In the big man's rage he was clumsy going for his gun and the smaller, far more agile man had covered the distance between them before the big man's gun had even cleared leather. Before a single shot could be fired Arkansas brought one of his Colts crashing down hard on the side of the big man's head, knocking him first senseless and then unconscious.

Arkansas bent and disarmed the fallen man. He looked at him for a moment, shook his head and then headed over to offices of the John Lance Cattle Company. The street, which had grown silent during the confrontation, was once more a frenzy of excited activity.

Arkansas kicked open the front door and stepped into the office. Lance was seated behind his desk with a man standing either side of him. Both men wore guns but neither went for them.

'I just left one of your men asleep in the street,' Arkansas told them. 'No doubt you were watching through the window.'

Lance looked perplexed. He gave a puzzled look to each of his men and then shrugged his shoulders and smiled.

Arkansas walked across to the desk and leaned over so that he was face to face with John Lance. The tension in the room was noticeable, almost a physical entity and both of Lance's men looked unsure of what to do. It was clear they felt the situation warranted guns, but Lance had obviously told them to hold their fire.

'Don't bother with the theatrics for my benefit. Just get your man off the street,' Arkansas said. 'The next man you send after me will come back dead.' He slammed Pug's guns down on the desk between them.

John Lance was finding it difficult to keep his usual composure. This man called Arkansas Smith had stepped over the line. Here he was in Lance's own office, his domain, and yet he was shouting the odds. The fact that Lance had two guns against his one didn't seem to bother him at all.

Lance stood up, not enjoying the way Arkansas was getting to him. The man seemed to have shifted the power of balance into his favour and the cattleman was not used to it. 'Look.' He pointed a finger at Arkansas. 'I don't know who you are or—'

'That's right,' Arkansas said, cutting the other man off mid speech. 'You don't know who I am, or, more to that point, *what* I am.'

Lance's eyes narrowed. 'What do you mean?'

'Consider yourself warned,' Arkansas said, and with

that he turned and left the offices with the intention of conducting his business with the sheriff. He didn't reach the sheriff's office though before the big man, having regained consciousness, challenged him once more.

'You slugged me, mister,' Pug said, and stood dead centre of the street, legs wide, arms hanging at his sides, hands curled inwards. Someone had given him another gunbelt and he looked ready to bring his gun into play with one upward movement.

'Don't be a fool,' Arkansas said. 'I'm tiring of you now.'

'Make your play,' the big man insisted. An angry bruise was forming on the side of his head where Arkansas had hit him. He was furious over that and knew that this was going to end one way only. There was no avoiding gunplay now that the point of no return had been crossed.

Arkansas stood perfectly still and allowed his eyes to scan the street. Onlookers had gathered and were watching with interest. John Lance was in the doorway of his offices and Rycot had emerged from the livery stable and was watching Arkansas closely, no doubt hoping to witness the fabled fast draw with his own eyes.

'Go for your gun,' Pug yelled, 'or I'll shoot you down anyway.'

'I don't want to hurt you,' Arkansas said, 'but I warn you I'll kill you this time.'

The coolness of the other man enraged Pug all the more and he snarled as he pulled his gun and shot, but his aim went wide, though the bullet did come perilously close to Arkansas's head and seemed to part his hair as it whistled past him.

Pug didn't get another chance before Arkansas's bullet took him in the stomach and spun him around before dropping him to the ground. He groaned in pain but still had some fight, if not sense, and he lifted the Colt, squaring it at Arkansas.

'No,' Arkansas said and shot again. This time the bullet took the big man dead centre of his forehead. His head snapped back sharply, sending a spray of crimson onto the air. His tongue slapped his face like fish guts hitting a sink. The last breath from his lungs closely followed and the final beat from his heart came just afterwards.

Arkansas looked across at Lance and shook his head. 'I warned you about this,' he said. 'You send another man after me and I'm going to send him back just as dead. And then I'm going to come after you.'

Coinciding with Arkansas's second shot, the sheriff emerged from his office and now he walked across the street and stood next to Arkansas. He watched as Arkansas holstered his weapon.

'I'll need to speak to you about this,' the lawman said.

'It's a small world,' Arkansas said, and calmly walked ahead of the sheriff towards his office.

NINE

The sheriff had been as much use as a hole in the head.

He had confirmed Lance's claims that he had purchased the McCord place legally from William McCord, but said he was not authorized to show the documents to any proxy of Mr McCord. On the subject of the doctor's disappearance, the sheriff had more or less implied that the doc did that from time to time. The only information of any use that Arkansas had gleaned from the lawman was that the name of the man left dead in the street was Pug Atkinson. The sheriff claimed to be unaware if the big man was working for Lance or not. And there was certainly no obvious connection between the shoot out and John Lance. 'Least, as far as the sheriff was concerned, there wasn't.

Arkansas didn't hold much credence in the sheriff's claims. It was obvious from the man's manner that the lawman was scared of John Lance and may have even been in his employ. Arkansas smelt a rat there, but it didn't really matter since he knew he would get to the bottom of it when he received the answer to his telegram.

There was no doubt in his mind that John Lance was talking through his hat regarding the purchase of Will's spread. It was also as sure as the wind blew that Lance had been responsible for Will's shooting. Maybe not directly, but he had at the very least ordered it. Arkansas felt he could place the man with the ornamental Colt at the scene and the fact that he worked for Lance was enough to press charges. Those charges would not stick without further evidence to back them up, but it was a start. Maybe he'd look up the man with the pretty gun.

Arkansas kept the sorrel at a steady pace. He felt no urgency to get back to the cabin.

He didn't think Lance would be loco enough to try anything at the moment, not after witnessing one of his men gunned down in the street. The cattleman claimed to have legal documents proving ownership of Will's place and when he came back it would be with the law at his side. Thing was, the man didn't realize that Arkansas was going to overrule that law.

The sorrel stumbled for a moment but then regained its steady pace and Arkansas patted the side of her head with a soothing hand. He spurred her forward and headed towards the cabin.

Will was dozing when he heard the sound but he snapped instantly awake. He grabbed the Spencer and worked its action, sending a shell into the chamber.

He listened but there was nothing. Not a sound and he relaxed slightly but then he heard it again.

Someone was rapping on the door.

He slowly swung his legs over and out of the bed and then gradually put his weight on them. A wave of pain shot through his stomach and he had to shift his weight back onto the bed. When he had left Arkansas had left the bedroom door open and Will could see through to the main door.

'Come in,' he shouted, and held the Spencer with the butt resting against his hip.

The knocking sounded again and Will frowned.

'Dammit, come in!' he yelled and winced when a fresh wave of pain sent molten lava coursing through his nervous system. Though the pain didn't last quite as long as before it still hurt like hell.

The door opened slowly and Will tensed, gritting his teeth against a secondary wave of pain as he pressed the rifle butt hard into his stomach. After what seemed an age a pretty face came around the door and then smiled when she saw him.

'I thought I'd check in on you,' Rebecca said, and entered the cabin and closed the door behind her. She was carrying a basket, the contents of which were covered with a thin tartan patterned cloth. 'I usually take my ride about this time of day so I thought I'd kill two birds with one stone.'

'Obliged,' Will said, and rested the Spencer on the bed. He managed to lift himself up slightly so that he was seated, legs hanging over the edge of the bed.

'You seem better,' Rebecca said.

'I'm on the mend,' Will agreed.

'I've baked some cakes for you and er—' She looked around the cabin.

'Arkansas,' Will said. 'He's gone into town on some business. Shouldn't be too long now.' He was sure he had seen a look of disappointment on the girl's face and he wondered if it really was *his* health that had prompted this visit.

Rebecca set the basket down on the table. 'You want for me to get you some coffce?' she asked.

'Sure,' Will said. He was feeling ravenous and guessed he must be getting some of his strength back. 'And one of those cakes would be good.' They were giving off a delicious aroma that set his mouth watering.

Rebecca smiled and disappeared from Will's view when she went to the stove. Arkansas had left the pot half full of coffee and Rebecca decided it was still fresh enough to drink and poured a little into a tin cup. She took it through to Will and sat down on the bed next to him.

'So, your friend?' Rebecca asked.

'Arkansas,' Will said, and took a bite out of one of the rock cakes. It was delicious, the pastry crumbling in his mouth.

'Arkansas,' she said. 'I've not seen him around these parts before.'

'No.' Will smiled. So it was interest in his friend that had brought her here and not his well-being. That was pretty much what he had expected. 'I've not seen him for years. He turned up a couple of days ago. Lucky for me he did.'

'Yes,' Rebecca agreed, and ran a hand over the bed to remove the crumbs Will had dropped. 'How did you get hurt?'

'Not too sure about that,' Will told her. 'Someone ran off my cattle and shot me. Rustlers maybe.'

'You're very lucky to have such a friend,' Rebecca said, and before Will could answer Arkansas came into the cabin and stood in the bedroom doorway. Neither of them had heard him ride up.

'Howdy.' He tipped his hat to them both. He was startled to find how glad he was to see the woman again. The feelings he was currently experiencing were alien to him and he didn't much understand them.

'Rebecca's made us some lovely cakes,' Will said. 'Make a nice change from your cooking. No offence, but you never were one with the pots and pans.'

'Obliged,' Arkansas said, and then turned to the woman. 'And after that dinner you cooked and all. Maybe you're trying to fatten us up,' he joked.

Rebecca blushed. 'I'll fix you some coffee,' she said, and quickly pushed past Arkansas and went to the stove.

It was a little after six and the first signs of night were visible in the sky. The sun was sinking into the mountains and sending a red sheen over the horizon. The sky seemed to be made up of a patchwork of vibrant colours – red, purple, even carmine in places. The diffused light danced across Rebecca's face and glittered in her eyes. It didn't seem possible but it made her even more beautiful.

Rebecca had said it was time she made a move and that her pa would worry about her if she didn't get home well before dark. It had been an enjoyable afternoon and after the men had polished off her cakes, Rebecca had made a delicious meat pie, which they had eaten with potatoes and a thick gravy made from the fats.

'I thank you for everything,' Arkansas said. He had escorted her outside and now they stood at the corral fence. 'I'm sure it's your care that's put Will on the mend so quickly.'

She smiled and once again her cheeks coloured as she blushed. For a moment she made eye contact with Arkansas and then self-consciously pulled her gaze away towards the far horizon. 'It's only neighbourly,' she said. 'We've been neighbours for some time, but until you brought my horse under control I don't think we ever shared more than a word when we passed each other in town. I never even knew his name nor that his place was so close to ours.'

'Where is your place?' Arkansas asked.

'I live a couple of miles yonder. My daddy owned the first ranch in this area. He came here long before Red Rock was a town.'

'And your ma?' Arkansas asked, and then wished he hadn't. Was he probing too deeply? Being too forward? In the West it just wasn't polite to ask too many questions.

Rebecca didn't seem to think so and a forlorn look

crossed her face. 'My mother died giving birth to me,' she told him. 'I was raised by my daddy.'

Arkansas smiled and nodded knowingly. He could understand her feelings of loss and how she must have felt growing up without knowing her own mother. He hadn't known his real parents and although he'd had a good upbringing by his adoptive parents, he had often felt a void deep inside himself that felt at times like a cavity in his soul. It was a need for identity that would always be there and would never be fulfilled.

'Life can be pretty cruel at times,' Arkansas said, after a long silence.

Rebecca nodded and turned towards her horse. She untied the reins from the fence and pulled it towards her.

'I may call tomorrow.'

'Sure,' Arkansas said. 'That would be nice.' He moved closer towards her and kissed her gently on the cheek and then stood back while she mounted her horse. He watched her ride off, waving and thinking that she was one of the finest women he had ever met.

TEN

'After I spoke to you in town I got to thinking and I went out looking for the doc,' Rycot said and had to catch his breath. 'Figured he couldn't be too far with my cart and all.'

'Figures,' Arkansas said and rolled himself a quirly.

'I very nearly missed him since some attempt has been made to hide the body, but I recognized a piece of lumber from my cart. When I found him he was dead,' Rycot said and then shook his head. 'I came straight here because the sheriff would be next to useless and you were closer in any case. I figured you'd want to know.'

Arkansas nodded and handed Rycot the whiskey bottle. 'Obliged.'

'They tried to hide the cart, too,' Rycot continued and took a slug from the bottle. 'Smashed it all to pieces. If I hadn't recognized that worm-eaten piece of lumber I wouldn't have found him.'

Rycot had come riding in not ten minutes ago, driving his horse as if he had the devil himself on his tail. It had taken him some time to catch his breath and now he slouched in a chair and and was swigging whiskey.

'Damn well shook me up,' Rycot said. 'Seeing the doc like that.' He shivered and made the sign of the cross with a finger upon his chest.

'It's too dark to go back out there now,' Arkansas said. 'You can stay here tonight, we'll head back out at first light.'

Rycot nodded and took another slug of the whiskey. 'Sure. Who do you think did for him?'

Arkansas shook his head. He had no real idea. It didn't make any scnse for Lance to be behind it: there would be no logical reason that he could see to do that to the doc.

Arkansas had a pretty good idea what Lance was up to. The documents detailing the sale of Will's spread would obviously be forgeries, so the attempt on Will's life made perfect sense. With Will out of the way Lance could just move right in and take control of the spread without his word being questioned. But his attempt to kill the man had failed. Now he'd have to produce the documents and deny Will's claims that they were forged. Arkansas hoped that the reason Lance was so keen to get his hands on Will's place would become clear when the answer to his telegram arrived in the morning. But whatever the reason, killing the doc would be a bizarre move for a man in John Lance's position.

It was then that the bedroom door opened and Will came out using the Spencer as a crutch. He gritted his teeth against his obvious pain and waved Arkansas away when he tried to come to his aid. He managed to reach a chair and sit himself down.

'What's happening?' Will asked.

'Howdy, Will,' Rycot said, and took another mouthful of the whiskey.

Will nodded at Rycot and then frowned. 'What in tar-nation's happening?'

Arkansas filled his friend in on recent events. Telling him about the gunfight in town and of how the doc had been missing since leaving here a few nights previously. Rycot had found him, the cart driven off the side of the road and the body partly buried with rocks. The doc had been shot in the chest. Rycot felt that the man would have died instantly.

'I don't understand what's going on here,' Will said, shaking his head. 'First someone tries to gun me down and now the doc. And Lance claims I sold this place to him. It makes no sense.'

'Lance will probably come up with a plausible reason for you denying selling to him,' Arkansas said. 'He claims to have documents signed by you.'

'I signed nothing for no man,' Will said.

Arkansas nodded. 'I'm mighty interested in seeing those documents.'

'John Lance is a rattlesnake,' Rycot contributed. 'I ain't never liked that man.'

'But why kill the doc?' Arkansas said and paced the room. 'If he has documents and it becomes his word against yours that the signature is forged, then killing the doc seems mighty stupid. And whatever John

Lance may be I don't think he's stupid.'

'Is that what you think?' Will asked. 'That Lance is behind it all?'

'I do,' Arkansas told him. 'I think he's forged your signature and that killing you and making it look like the work of rustlers took away the possibility of you disputing his claims. Or it would have if he had actually killed you. Now he's just going to have to face you down, claim that you are trying to backtrack on the deal. I just can't figure out any good reason to gun the doctor down. If anything that's plumb loco.'

'Someone killed him,' Rycot said. His eyes had glazed over and the whiskey bottle was getting close to being dry. 'That much I can tell you.'

'I don't think it was Lance, though,' Arkansas said. ' 'Less he's loco, a mad dog.'

'Then who?' Will grimaced and clutched his side as he felt a fresh wave of pain.

'That's what I aim to find out,' Arkansas said. He took the makings from his shirt pocket and rolled and lit a quirly.

ELEVEN

Sheriff Bill Hackman was a troubled man.

He'd hardly slept all night and, as the dawn broke, he suddenly felt exhausted. The little rest he had managed had hardly been reviving and he groaned as he worked a kink out of his back. Recent events were catching up with him and although only fifty years old he felt every one of those years tenfold.

He left the jailhouse, figuring he might as well patrol the town before the bustle of the day started. It would be impossible to snatch any sleep now that the day had arrived and even if he did get a chance, a quiet few hours, his mind would refuse to switch off.

Lance had been livid about the gunfight between Pug and the man called Arkansas Smith. He had demanded Smith be arrested, but the sheriff told him that was out of the question. It was a fair fight and half the town had witnessed it – dammit, he'd witnessed it himself. There was nothing the law could do, not even a law that belonged to John Lance. The arrival of this Arkansas Smith had certainly ruffled a few feathers and was continuing to do so. He had a reputation as a gunslinger, a man who hired out his skills to the highest bidder. Why he was in Red Rock was beyond the lawman. And what exactly was his connection to William McCord?

The sheriff was just about to turn out of Main Street when he heard the arrival of riders coming into town from the south. He turned and saw them, two men, riding side by side. As they neared he could make out the thunder both seemed to carry in their faces. He recognized them both: one was Rycot and the other was the man called Arkansas Smith.

'Sheriff,' Arkansas said, as they pulled their horses to a stop a few feet from the lawman. 'About four miles out of town, where the road forks off towards the mountains you'll find the doc.'

The sheriff looked perplexed and he shrugged his shoulders. Drunken doctors were hardy his bailiwick.

'He's dead.'

The sheriff looked first at Rycot and then at Arkansas. 'Dead?' he said, his mouth suddenly dry. 'How?'

'Shot,' Arkansas said. 'By person or persons unknown. They tried to hide the body but Mr Rycot here's a bloodhound. The cart the doc was driving was forced off the road and into the bushes, but Rycot spotted it.'

Rycot seemed to like that and he tipped his hat to the sheriff. 'Recognized a piece of my cart. When you catch these skunks I hope the law will compensate me. That cart was not more than a year old.' In truth, the cart was long past its best and only fit for firewood, but Rycot figured he was due some remuneration for his troubles.

'I'll get some men together and ride out there straight away,' the sheriff told them.

'You do that,' Arkansas said. 'I'll be needing to speak to you later.' He turned his horse and started towards Rycot's livery stable, leaving the sheriff staring at their backs as they crossed the street.

'What time will the telegraph office open?' Arkansas asked.

Rycot scratched his head. 'Nine, I think. Takes a little while for most folk in this town to get going of a morning.' He obviously didn't have much use for such modern contraptions as telegrams.

Arkansas looked up at the sun. 'Just over an hour,' he said, and then smiled at Rycot. 'You got coffee making facilities in that livery of yours?'

'Sure,' Rycot said, proudly.

'Then get some brewing.' Arkansas dismounted and led his horse into a stall. He threw some fresh grain into the trough and his horse went at it immediately.

'Yes sir.' The telegraph operator responded to Arkansas's query and quickly crossed the room and grabbed two sheets of paper from a pigeonhole. 'They arrived promptly this morning.' He handed the sheets over.

Arkansas quickly ran an eye over both sheets, a thin smile forming at the corners of his mouth.

'Obliged,' he said and tipped his hat. He walked out of the small telegraph office to where Rycot waited for him on the sidewalk.

'Did it come?'

Arkansas stuffed the sheets into his pocket. 'Sure did.'

'Well, what's so all-fire important?'

Arkansas smiled. Rycot seemed to have elected himself his pard. He decided to counter the question with another question rather than be evasive.

'Is the sheriff back yet?'

Rycot shook his head.

'No matter,' Arkansas said. 'I'll catch up with him on the way back to Will's.'

'You want I should come with you?' Rycot asked. 'Having another man around may prove helpful with your pard still on the mend.'

'Sure.' Arkansas nodded, knowing that from here on in things could get a little tricky. Having another gun around would not do any harm. And besides, Arkansas had a theory he wanted to check out and leaving someone behind with Will seemed prudent. The telegram had offered no obvious reason for Lance's desire to get his hands on Will's spread but the rancher had acquired some properties in recent months and Arkansas had a hunch. He always played his hunches and more than once it had been an intuition, a strange feeling, which had saved his life.

They went across to the livery and readied their horses. Before they mounted up and left for Will's place, Rycot hung a sign over the door saying that he was closed for a few days but anyone using the stable should leave a signed IOU.

Both men were oblivious to that fact that across the street, John Lance stood in his office window watching them and he continued to do so as they started their horses out of town.

They had gone perhaps a mile when they saw the sheriff and half-a-dozen other riders coming towards them.

TWELVE

Doc Cooter's body was covered in a saddle blanket and draped across a horse that was tied behind the sheriff's mount. All of the riders looked grim faced as they pulled their horses to a stop.

'You found him then?' Arkansas stated the obvious and sucked at his quirly. He allowed the smoke to drift out of the corners of his mouth as he steadied his horse.

The sheriff nodded. He eyes went first from Arkansas to Rycot and then over his shoulder to the body of the unfortunate doctor. 'Either of you got any idea who did this?'

'Some,' Arkansas said.

'Care to share with me?' The sheriff was trying to sound tough, in control, but there was a tremor in his voice. He was obviously ill at ease up against a man with Arkansas's reputation.

Arkansas shook his head. 'When I know for certain,' he said, 'you'll be the first to know.'

The sheriff nodded and kicked his horse into

movement. The rest of the posse followed. They hadn't gone more than a dozen feet when Arkansas turned over his shoulder and called the sheriff.

'Yeah?' The sheriff looked back at him, his expression, weary, hangdog.

'When you come out to Will's place with Lance to take possession, best make sure your papers are legal and in order,' Arkansas said, and winked at Rycot, though the old man could fathom no meaning in the gesture.

The sheriff merely nodded and led the posse back to town with their grim cargo.

'Because I've got some legal papers all of my own,' Arkansas mumbled, and then rode off with Rycot in tow.

Arkansas felt better at leaving Will now that Rycot had taken up the position of companion and guard. They were both armed with rifles that belonged to Rycot, so Arkansas had brought his own Spencer with him. Things went a certain way, he might end up having to use it. He kept the sorrel at a steady pace. His destination was less than six miles away, but there was a lot of rough ground between here and there and he didn't want to strain the animal. Before he had left, Will had given him a map of the general area and the Bowen place was clearly marked. He would have no trouble finding it.

The telegrams he had received were nestled snugly in his pocket. The first came directly from the territorial governor's office and stated that Arkansas

Smith was acting on behalf of the US Government and had full legal powers. The second came from the land registration office and could show no reason for John Lance to be interested in Will's land claim. Land could suddenly prove valuable if needed for the railroad's extension across the West, but no plans were evident for the railroad to come anywhere near Red Rock. There was also no chance of the land in this area containing any precious minerals. Lance's desire for Will's place was a mystery. The telegram also informed Arkansas that John Lance had acquired several ranches over the last twelve months, bought from the owners at less than the current market value. One man had cried foul and claimed that he had been swindled out of his spread but he'd vanished shortly afterwards and his claims were never followed up. That property, once owned by Clive Bowen, an Irish immigrant, was now under Lance's ownership but was reportedly lying empty.

Rycot had known the place and had also known old man Bowen. He'd said his disappearance was a mystery that still troubled him and he hated to think of Bowen lying dead somewhere in a shallow and unmarked grave. Done for, the way the doc had been.

If Arkansas was to tie Lance into Will's shooting then he needed to find the owner of the ornately handled knife and his partner. But neither of the men had been seen around town lately and it was certain that they were hiding out somewhere. Arkansas doubted that Lance would be stupid enough to keep them too close. It made perfect sense for them to be hiding out at the Bowen place since it seemed to be the only one of Lance's extensive list of properties that was standing empty. It was also far enough away from Red Rock, and off the beaten track, for someone to keep away from attention.

Least that was the hunch and Arkansas, true to form, was playing it.

YESTERYEAR

Arkansas stared across the desk at the curious-looking man with the head that was almost perfectly dome-shaped Everything about the man was globular – a rotund head, sunk into a podgy neck which sat atop a pair of rounded shoulders. His belly ballooned out over his belt like some great fleshy ball and his legs bulged at the knees forming a half circle.

'You've got me at a disadvantage,' Arkansas said. 'You know my name and I don't seem to recall yours.' The chains around Arkansas's wrists were biting into the skin but he ignored the pain. The chain ran downwards alongside his legs and was attached to the heavy shackles he wore.

'I'm Justice O'Keefe,' the man said. He adjusted the tie slightly and ran a finger behind his ill-fitting collar as though struggling for air. 'And you – once a Texas Ranger, a war hero, and now just a common criminal. A killer, no less, who has an appointment at dawn with the rope. What a disappointment.'

'I'm none too pleased about it myself.'

The portly man smiled. 'Good to keep a sense of humour,'

89

he said. 'It'll be of comfort on your way to the gallows.'

'Look,' Arkansas snarled, tensing and pulling at his chains, but O'Keefe didn't move. He was in no danger. There was no way for Arkansas to break free of his bindings, but all the same the sheriff came back into the room, alerted at the sound of the struggle, his Army Model Colt in hand.

'Please remain outside, Sheriff,' O'Keefe said. He was clearly in control of the situation and was in no need of assistance.

For a moment the sheriff looked unsure and his face held a puzzled expression that almost looked pained. 'If this skunk gives you trouble,' he said, eventually, 'I'll plug him here and now. Bullet or rope – he'll still be very much dead.'

'Thank you,' said O'Keefe. 'I'll keep that in mind. Now, if you'll excuse us, please.'

The sheriff shrugged his shoulders and left the room, slamming the heavy door behind him.

'You see,' O'Keefe said, 'unpleasant fellow.'

'What do you want with me?' Arkansas asked.

'I think I can help you.'

Arkansas looked the man directly in the eye. 'You talking about my heavenly soul? I've had enough with the praying already and I'll meet my Maker on my own terms.'

'I'm talking very much about the physical you. What eventually happens to your soul is none of my concern.'

'I'm listening.'

'I represent Washington,' O'Keefe told him. 'We've been following your little rampage with great interest.'

'Then you'll know I'm here on trumped-up charges,' Arkansas said. 'That those men deserved to die.'

'Difficult to prove, though.' The podgy man pulled a large

cigar from his coat and took a match to it. He sucked hard on the thick tobacco. 'In fact, with the amount of corruption around here I would say it's impossible to prove. And whichever way you look at it, the fact remains that you killed those six men, four of whom were US Calvary, not to mention a prominent politician and his son.'

'And I'd do it again.' Defiantly, words spat out with real venom. 'To a man those lot were skunks. They shouldn't have done what they did.'

'Tell me,' asked O'Keefe, pacing the small room, 'have you ever heard of the Pinkertons?'

'Alan Pinkerton?' Arkansas said, resenting the fact that O'Keefe was talking down to him, as if he were dumb. He was lettered and he read whatever he could get his hands on. 'Started up his agency when Pinkerton foiled an assassination attempt on President Lincoln. They protected the President during the war. I met a Pinkerton once – rat-faced-looking guy. Can't say I really took to him.'

'They still protect the current President,' O'Keefe said. 'But they can't be everywhere at all times and, since the war, the area west of the Mississippi is proving problematic. Which is where you come in.'

'Go on.'

'I represent the President himself and I've been given the task of forming a special force. A team of ten agents all working independently of each other to enforce the law in this increasingly hostile landscape. Civilization is coming to the West and we need men out there to do the civilizing. Men like Arkansas Smith, men who know the land, men of courage.'

'But I'm a convicted killer?' Arkansas pointed out, as if the fact had slipped the man's mind. 'Due to hang at dawn.'

'Oh, that,' O'Keefe said it as though it were a trifling matter of no real onsequence. 'Are you willing to enlist with us? To sign on and take orders directly from me? You'll have the powers of a territorial marshal and more besides. Seems to me you have a simple choice: join us or swing.'

'Why do I feel as if I'm going to put a tighter rope around my neck than the one waiting for me?'

O'Keefe smiled. 'Because you are perceptive, Mr Smith,' he said, and left the room to make the necessary arrangements.

THIRTEEN

Seemed the hunch paid off. Not that he had ever doubted it, but Arkansas had a feeling of incredible fortitude as he pulled the sorrel into the bushes that grew the length of a natural banking above the Bowen ranch house. He tethered the horse to a thick branch and then crawled out of the bushes and lay prone on the ground.

The ranch house was an adobe building typical of most other properties in the area, though there were some concessions to the western style with a gable roof and a frame porch. A thin trail of wood smoke drifted out of the chimney and Arkansas lay there for some time, watching. There was someone in there. Didn't have to be the men called Clay and Jim but somehow Arkansas knew it would turn out to be them.

That hunch again.

After a while with no sign of movement he decided he'd have to go down, sneak up on the place and find out for sure how many men were in there before he made a move. He went back to the sorrel and pulled his Spencer from the saddle boot and then started down the banking. He tried to keep himself behind cover as much as possible and he was almost at the foot of the banking before he found he needed to break cover.

There was a stone well halfway between the banking and the house and Arkansas ran for it and then bent down, resting a moment with the stone structure hiding him from view of anyone in the house. He worked the action on the Spencer and checked his Colt – there was no real need to do so since he'd done it twice already, but, like his hunches, he had his own little quirks.

He sat there for some time, his own breathing sounding impossibly loud. For a moment he thought he heard faint voices drifting from the house but he decided it must have been his imagination. He scooped up a few stones, stood up and pelted them at the door. They struck true to aim and he lifted the Spencer and pointed it directly at the door.

The door opened and Arkansas recognized the man as one of those he'd met in town – the man called Clay.

Once again one of Arkansas's hunches had struck pay dirt.

The man was wearing the ornate handled Colt, the close relation to the knife Arkansas carried in his waistband. There was no sign of the other man, the one called Jim. If he was in there he didn't come to the door and Arkansas's eyes scanned the entire area, ready for a shot out of concealment.

Clay wore his gun down low on his hip and his hand coiled, over it. He was clearly battling with himself over his chances if he made a play.

'I wouldn't,' Arkansas said. 'Where's your friend?'

'Ain't got no friends,' Clay shouted back.

'That's a nice weapon.' Arkansas pointed the eye of his rifle at the man's gun belt. 'Very pretty.'

The man stood perfectly rigid, unsure of where this was heading.

'Loosen your belt,' Arkansas ordered, 'slowly, and then toss it into the dirt towards me. I'm a dead shot with this Spencer and it's aimed directly between your eyes – no sudden moves, or I'll blow your head clean into the next territory.'

Clay's hand went to the clasp of his belt in a ridiculously slow movement. He paused for a second, seemingly calculating his chances were he to draw, but then deciding that the odds were not to his liking he released the clasp. He pulled the belt slowly around his waist and let it hang like a rattler from his hand.

'Toss it,' Arkansas said.

Clay did so, throwing the belt some ten feet in front of him.

'Where's your pard?' Arkansas asked.

'I told you,' Clay said, 'I ain't got no friends.'

Arkansas shot and then quickly worked the action on the Spencer, sending another bullet into the breech.

Clay let out a scream as the bullet powered into the door frame barely inches from his head. Wood splinters and dust hit the side of his face and the smell of cordite struck his nostrils like the putrid aroma of hell.

'I'm alone,' Clay shouted in genuine terror. 'Jim rode out this morning. He's hunting and could be gone all day.'

Keeping the rifle levelled at Clay, Arkansas carefully stepped around the well and walked directly towards the man. Fully aware of what was happening around him, he took steady calculated steps. The shot of only seconds ago would bring the other man running if he was within range of the sound and Arkansas didn't want be surprised by his arrival. He reached the discarded gunbelt and bent his knees, keeping the rifle aimed at Clay, and slid the ornate Colt from the leather.

Arkansas lowered the rifle while he probed in his pocket and retrieved the knife. 'Snap,' he said, holding the knife and Colt in the one hand and resting the butt of the rifle on his hip.

'Where'd you—?' The question ended abruptly as Clay realized where Arkansas had got the knife from and what it meant.

'Give me one reason why I shouldn't kill you here and now,' Arkansas snarled.

'Weren't me shot your friend,' Clay said, his voice heavy with fear.

'You were there. Else how do you explain this knife?'

'I was there,' Clay agreed and then pleaded, 'Weren't me that shot him, though.'

'Who shot the doc?' Arkansas's finger tightened on

the trigger, just enough for the other man to notice it.

'That was an accident,' Clay said quickly and held his hands out before him as if they would protect him from the rifle.

'Accident?'

'We, my pard and me, were trying to get information out of him regarding your friend. If he was going to make it and such like. He wouldn't talk. We waved the gun about to frighten him. That's all.' As he spoke, Clay's shoulders slumped forward and he had to swallow hard to stop himself gibbering like the yellow coward he was. 'The damn thing went off. It was an accident.'

Arkansas walked slowly towards Clay, keeping his eyes directly into the other man's. He could see the sweat on Clay's face and his muscles twitching in fear.

'Please,' Clay pleaded, 'weren't my fault. Only meant to scare the doc a little.'

'What about Will?' Arkansas snarled. 'Did you mean to just scare him too?'

'Please, mister, I had no choice. I just do what I'm told.'

Arkansas smiled. That's what he wanted to hear. There was of course more to come but that would do for now. The cowboy was scared, terrified and would talk volumes as long as he thought it would keep him alive.

'By John Lance?'

Clay's shoulders shrugged and he nodded. 'Yes.'

Arkansas drew level with Clay and his smile broadened. The gesture seemed to terrify the man even further and his pants gave away the fact that he had just that second lost control of his bladder. Then, like a sudden flash of lightning in a clement sky, without warning Arkansas swung the rifle wide and brought the stock crashing in a powerful blow to the side of Clay's face.

Clay let out a small yelp that could have come from a puppy dog and then his eyes rolled back in their sockets, his legs buckled beneath him and he fell to the ground unconscious.

Arkansas took a quick look around him but still there was no sign of the other man, the one called Jim. He bent and quickly dragged Clay into the house. He'd tie and gag the man and then get his own horse and hide it out of sight in one of the many outbuildings.

He figured he wouldn't have to wait too long for Jim to return.

FOURTEEN

It was getting perilously close to sundown and still the other man had not returned to the small ranch house. Arkansas wasn't comfortable with this development, or rather the lack of any real development whatsoever.

He didn't want to be away from Will's place overnight. The fact that Rycot was there made him feel a little easier, but with Lance due to ride in come dawn and attempt to take possession of the spread, he figured he'd better be there. Rycot seemed a good man, but Will was still on the mend and not up to a fight of any kind. No, he had to be there when Lance came with his fake papers and, no doubt, a heavily armed gang of men to back him up.

He was the only one who could stop John Lance and he was going to stop him: there was no question of that.

It had been a productive afternoon and Clay had sung like a bird. As soon as the man had regained consciousness and found his arms and feet bound with thick rawhide, Arkansas had started to question him. Initially the man had been reluctant to talk, but Arkansas had used the ornately decorated knife to persuade him.

'Course Arkansas didn't have it in him to coldly slice a man up, to torture him with expertly placed slashes of the flesh designed to cause the maximum pain, but that didn't matter. The fact that Clay had thought Arkansas capable of such depravity had done the trick. All Arkansas had to do to loosen the man's tongue was effect a cruel stare and allow the blade to briefly touch the man's flesh.

The attack on Will's place had been on Lance's orders. Clay had been there, together with his partner Jim, and several other men in Lance's employ. The other men had run Will's stock off while Clay and Jim ransacked the house. It was at that point in the telling that Clay became visibly agitated and the wet patch in his pants widened. He pleaded that he had not wanted to shoot Will, neither had Jim, but if they didn't carry out their boss's orders they would be shot themselves.

They'd had no choice. Arkansas had to understand that.

The doc had been an accident and nothing to do with John Lance. They, Jim and himself, figured on finding out what the doc had been doing at Will's place and if indeed Will was alive or dead. Trouble was, the doc had come over all spunky and refused to tell them anything. They had been trying to scare him when the gun went off. Clay claimed that it was Jim whose finger had been on the trigger.

That last point was moot to Arkansas. In his opinion

both men were as guilty as each other. He had assured Clay that if he testified to all this in a court he would be protected and, after a short jail term, be allowed to start again. The man wasn't stupid and he realized that he was out of options. He nodded before breaking into tears and sobbing like a baby.

And now Clay was lying in the corner of the room, legs and arms still bound and a gag forced into his mouth. Whilst he had been co-operative thus far, Arkansas wasn't going to take a chance of him screaming out and alerting his pard.

If the other man ever showed up that was.

Arkansas rolled and lit himself a quirly. He glanced out of the window at the horizon but there was no sign of anyone out there.

There were a number of possibilities for Jim failing to show up. Had he returned before Arkansas had hidden his horse away in one of the outbuildings and then fled before being noticed? Or was he simply taking his time with his hunting trip, going on till nightfall, chasing after some elusive prey?

Arkansas suspected the second option was the more likely.

He also knew that there was no way he'd wait until nightfall for the other man.

No, he'd have to leave now, take Clay with him. He'd have to get the man into Red Rock and then, after showing the sheriff his authorization papers, get Clay locked away. He suspected the sheriff and Lance were too close and that the lawman was not to be trusted, but Arkansas didn't think the sheriff would go against him when he saw the legal papers he held.

He didn't like leaving Jim out there, loose ends were to be avoided and he would have much preferred to lead both men into town, but there was little choice. It was unlikely that Will and Rycot were in any immediate danger, but if Jim had returned and saw him here and then ridden on and informed Lance, then things could get mighty tricky.

Would Lance panic that Arkansas seemed to be getting closer to him and ride out with a heavily armed gang to Will's place for a showdown? That wasn't a chance Arkansas wanted to take.

'No choice about it,' he said and looked at Clay.

The bound man mumbled something beneath his gag.

'Guess I'm taking you into town,' Arkansas told him.

He crossed the room and peered through the window once more but again all he was greeted with was the glorious never-ending landscape. 'Don't worry, Lance won't get at you. I'll make sure of that.'

Clay nodded and this time didn't even bother to mumble.

'I'm going to get the horses,' Arkansas said. 'You stay there and shut up and I'll untie you when I come back.'

Clay did all he could do and simply nodded.

Arkansas led his sorrel and a black mustang to the ranch house and tethered both animals to the hitching rail. Once again he scanned the horizon for Jim and once more saw nothing, before going back into the house.

He took the ornate knife and sliced the bindings at Clay's feet. He left Clay's hands tied and then, before removing the gag, he pulled one of his Colts and pointed it directly into the man's face.

'Don't try anything stupid,' Arkansas warned. 'Just like with the doc my gun could go off by accident if I stumble. 'Course if that happens then you won't be around to know about it.'

'Mister,' Clay said, gasping for air, 'I'm through with stupid things.'

'Good to hear it,' Arkansas said. 'Now, up.' He grabbed Clay's still bound wrists and pulled him to his feet. He allowed the man to bend and straighten each leg in turn to work the cramp from his muscles. 'Remember, nothing stupid, 'he reminded the man.

Arkansas grabbed his Spencer and then placed the Colt back into leather. He prodded the barrel of the rifle into Clay's back and pushed him towards the door.

'Slowly,' he said.

Clay moved on ahead – carefully, feeling the gun in his back with each step. He certainly wasn't going to give any trouble and seemed terrified of the man with the rifle.

Once outside he paused on the stoop.

'Make your way to your horse,' Arkansas ordered. 'I'll help you mount up.'

Clay reached his horse and stood beside the mustang.

Again Arkansas removed a Colt and lowered the

rifle to the ground. 'Now, no funny ideas,' he said. 'I'm gonna' give you a foot up onto your horse and then bind your hands to the saddle horn. One wrong move and I'll put a slug straight in the small of your back. At this range it'll tear your organs apart. You'll die quickly but it'll be painful.'

'Just get me on my horse.' Clay said. 'I don't want to hear none of that kind of talk.'

Arkansas bent his knees and grabbed Clay by the back of his waist band. He lifted while the other man swung his legs over the horse.

The shot came from nowhere: breaking the afternoon air like a crack in the sky itself.

Arkansas hit the ground hard and grabbed the Spencer. He rolled and came up in a crouch, rifle ready to fire, eyes scanning for the shooter. There was another shot and Arkansas saw the rifle flash and let one off in that direction before running back for the doorway to the house.

At the sound of the first shot the mustang had bucked but had been unable to break free of its reins and it remained tethered to the hitch rail. Clay lay there, half on the horse and half off. He was completely motionless and Arkansas didn't have to get any closer to know that the man had died. The way his lifeless eyes stared back at him told him that. Jim had returned and, crack shot hunter that he was, had missed his intended target and killed his pard.

'Damn,' Arkansas spat. With Clay dead his witness had gone and the case he had built against Lance had been instantly destroyed with the violent crack of gunfire. He poked his head around the doorway and fired a shot in the general direction of where he figured Jim was hiding.

There was fire in return and then Arkansas heard the sound of galloping hoofs. The man was attempting to flee, no doubt riding to warn John Lance that things were moving up a step or two.

'Shit,' Arkansas cursed and ran out of the house and quickly mounted the sorrel. He didn't bother checking on Clay – the man was dead. Arkansas figured his first priority was in catching up with the other man.

He spurred the horse into action and set off in pursuit of the myopic man called Jim.

FIFTEEN

The chase was hopeless.

Jim had too much of a head start and his horse seemed to move like the wind and had no problem keeping up its pace over the rocky terrain, but all was not lost. The great many years Arkansas had spent with the Rangers had turned him into an expert tracker, he could read the trail as other men would read a book. Not that he needed to since the tracks were fresh and Jim was pushing his horse to the limit and was making no attempt to cover up his tracks.

Arkansas hung back and allowed the other man to vanish from sight, figuring he'd stay at a distance until he was good and ready to attack. And, besides, he had a good idea where the man called Jim was heading. He didn't have to check the map in his pocket to figure the man was riding towards Lance's place.

Maybe the best option would be to allow the man to get there and then ride in and confront him. It would be dangerous with all the firepower Lance would have around him, but Arkansas didn't figure any of them had the stomach for a real fight. The way he saw it John Lance was a small-town businessman with tendencies to bully those around him. He relied on his men and the ever-present threat of violence to get his way but would fall apart against an opposition prepared to fight back. An opponent like Arkansas Smith, a man who had lived his entire life dodging one bullet or another, would be too much for Lance and his crew of cowboys.

Intelligence certainly wasn't Lance's men's strongpoint. Killing the doc had served no purpose and the attack on Will had been clumsily executed. If the men had known what they were doing and killed Will, then there would be no way to disprove Lance's claim of ownership of Will's spread.

Arkansas had it all pretty much worked out, but there was one thing that still puzzled him. What was so important about Will's place? What was it that made Lance want it so badly that he was prepared to send his men out to kill? And forging documents of sale would take some doing.

Although Arkansas hadn't seen the papers as of yet, he assumed they would look legal enough with Will's signature forged professionally. 'Course if Lance had had his way and Will had died in the attack then the rancher could have taken over the spread all sweet and dandy.

'Things often don't work out as planned,' Arkansas answered his thoughts aloud and took the sorrel over a bluff.

In the distance he could see the dust trail thrown

up by Jim's horse. He figured the man was maybe a mile or so ahead of him, but in this wide-open country he would have to be a lot further away to have vanished from sight. On a clear day a man could look out over the open plains and see for many miles in all directions.

Yep, no doubt about it – the cowboy was heading for John Lance's place.

'Your pard's been some time,' Rycot pointed out, and handed the whiskey bottle to Will.

Will took a slug and then smiled. 'He'll be back.'

'You so sure?'

'I am,' Will said. 'I've known that boy a long time and I don't think the varmint's been born who can take him on and come out on top.'

'How long you known him then?' Rycot asked, genuinely interested. He leaned forward on the upturned bucket he was using for a seat and stared at the other man. He smiled meekly as he leaned forward to break wind.

Will moved and winced at the pain in his side. Still, he was already better than he had any right to be and he managed to cross the room and sit himself down in the soft chair. There was an unpleasant smell coming from Rycot and no amount of pain would stop Will moving to the other side of the room.

'We were Rangers together,' Will said. 'We saw a lot of action, fought a lot of fights.' For a moment his eyes seemed to cloud over as he peered through the mist of the years to locate the memories. 'Indians – we must have fought every type of Indian there is at one time or another. We chased outlaws and Mexican bandits right across Texas and into territories that weren't even named then. They were good days. Back then I never thought I'd get old but it soon caught up with me.'

'The Texas Rangers?' Rycot leaned for the whiskey bottle. He farted again and cursed the beans and jerky they'd shared for lunch.

Will nodded and carefully made himself a quirly before speaking.

'Arkansas was nothing more than a kid when I first met him and I, being the veteran man, took him under my wing. The first time I saw him shoot you could have pushed me over with a twig. Never did see anyone who could shoot the way that boy shoots. Don't think he really had much of a childhood since he was orphaned in an Indian attack and the folks who raised him died when he was still young. I think he must have been fending for himself when he was still a kid. He grew up kinda tough.'

'There are lots of stories about him,' Rycot said. 'That's he's an outlaw, a bounty hunter, a mudsill. Some even say he's some kind of special lawman with powers that take him all over the West.'

Will nodded. He knew the stories, the legends. A couple of years ago some shoddy hack writer had spent some time with Arkansas and then produced a dime novel – *The King of the Colt* by G.M. Dobbs. The writer, a green-horn Easterner with far too much imagination and little real facts, had filled the book with sensationalist scuttlebutt. Will doubted any of it was true. 'Course the fact that the book had been a massive success meant that the name Arkansas Smith had the same recognition as any of the legendary lawmen and outlaws who populate the West.

'I know what they all say,' Will remarked. 'Don't believe much of it myself.'

'You don't think he's an outlaw?'

'Hell, no.'

'A lawman, then?'

Will looked at Rycot and then smiled. 'I don't rightly know. I ain't seen him for a good few years. At one point I'd heard he'd been hanged for killing three men down in Reno.'

'That sure enough ain't so.'

Will laughed. 'The only thing I know for certain,' Will said, 'is that he was once a damn good Texas Ranger, anything else is all fancy frills.'

'I heard he once fought off three Mexican bandits with only two bullets in his gun. The second bullet went straight through one man and into the other,' Rycot said, quoting a story that filled an entire chapter of the dime novel that purported to tell the true story of Arkansas's life.

Will smiled. 'Let me tell you something,' he said. 'That damn book tells of how Ark wrestled a grizzly with his bare hands. That ain't true for one thing because Ark's terrified of grizzlies. I once seem him run clean across the Pecos screaming like a two-bit whore with a bear snarling after him. He was too scared to take aim at the beast, let along engage it in hand-to-hand combat.'

Rycot stood up and worked a kink out of his back. He walked over to the window and looked at the crimson coloured sky.

'Be dark soon,' he said – and farted again.

SIXTEEN

Arkansas brought the horse to a halt as he reached the boundaries of the Lance property. In the distance he could see the large ranch house and the outbuildings. It certainly looked an impressive spread. The outbuildings alone, all built in a mixture of the Spanish and American styles, looked more comfortable than most houses he had ever seen.

Damn, he'd never even stayed in a house as fancy as those outbuildings.

Jim must have already ridden into the property since Arkansas had not seen hide nor hair of him for the last couple of miles, but his tracks were clear enough. Arkansas patted the side of the sorrel's head and whispered comforts to it while he decided what to do next.

Night was still being held away by the remnants of the evening, but the sky was cobalt and the temperature had dropped a few degrees. And Arkansas was desperate to get back to Will's place before nightfall.

For a moment he thought of Clay, laying there dead back at the old Bowen place, killed by a stray bullet and the doc supposedly shot by accident. Each of those deaths were the responsibility of John Lance. And what of the man called Pug who had provoked and lost a gunfight with Arkansas? And, of course, there was old man Bowen who had mysteriously disappeared. Was he another victim of Lance's empire building? Not to mention Will who, too, would have been dead were it not for a stroke of luck when the bullet failed to destroy any vital organs and got snagged up in thick fatty tissue.

'Come on,' Arkansas said to the horse and started it slowly towards the ranch. He wasn't sure what he exactly intended to do, but he knew he had to confront Lance. He realized how foolish it was to ride in by himself – effectively into a hornets' nest. He was one gun, a crack-shot maybe, but still only one against many. He'd faced greater odds in the past, though.

Arkansas was counting on the fact that John Lance wouldn't go up against him on the spur of the moment, that the rancher was too devious for that and would prefer to attack later, preferably when he (Lance) was far away and could not be implicated in events. The man was a coward and, if anything, that made him all the more dangerous. You knew where you were with a fighting man, but a coward would come at you from behind or when you were asleep. A coward would strike at those close to you, cowards had all the moral boundaries of a gutter rat.

Arkansas didn't much like cowards.

As he neared the ranch Arkansas saw a group of men standing immediately outside the grand ranch house, John Lance was at the head of the group. He quickly scanned the faces but there was no sign of the man called Jim.

Arkansas pulled his horse to a halt outside the ranch gates and waited, saying nothing.

John Lance, flanked by several armed men, walked towards him.

'What can I do for you?' Lance asked.

Arkansas smiled. 'Tell your men that anyone so much as moves I'll kill them stone dead.'

'Brave talk for a lone man,' Lance said.

'Try me.' The words had a dread about them that hung heavy in the air and caused more than one of Lance's men to twitch involuntarily.

'Why would we want to hurt you?' Lance asked. 'I'm am a peaceable rancher.'

'You're a low-down, lying varmint is what you are,' Arkansas told him and shifted casually in his saddle.

Briefly Lance was angered but he managed to pull himself under control.

'State your business,' he said, firmly. He didn't want to lose face in front of his men and he was damned if he'd show any physical signs that the man called Arkansas Smith worried him.

'My business,' Arkansas said, 'is to see you hang.'

Lance was taken aback and he produced a large cigar from his pocket and struck a match to it. He looked ill at ease as he smoked and it was obvious from his manner that he was struggling to remain calm. He drew heavily on the cigar and allowed the smoke to twist between his teeth.

'One of your men, goes by the name of Jim, rode in here not too long ago,' Arkansas said.

'Did he?' Lance spoke through a thick plume of smoke.

'He did,' Arkansas said. 'Him and his pard, a man known as Clay, killed the doc. Clay's dead himself. Shot by his short-sighted pard. He's lying back at the old Bowen place.'

'The doc?' Lance was genuinely surprised. Maybe he had nothing to do with that, but either way he obviously had not yet had a chance to talk to Jim.

'They were both among the gang that shot William McCord – men acting on your orders. Killing the doc they did on their own initiative, or so it seems. And the man called Pug that I gunned down in Red Rock. You forced that fight on me. You couldn't be any more responsible if you'd pulled the trigger yourself.'

'Well,' Lance said. 'That's a mighty dandy tall tale, but I've got no time for this. But for the record I don't know any men called Jim and Clay, but if there is a dead man back at the Bowen place then that concerns me. That's my property now and as for the doc—'

Arkansas cut Lance off mid speech when he pointed a finger directly at the man.

'Cut the hogwash,' he said. 'I know what you are and I know the bill of sale you have for Will's place is a forgery.'

'I don't much like your tone, mister,' Lance said, obviously having given up any attempt to hold his back his anger. 'I bought McCord's property fair and square. Now I'm a law-abiding man, but as from dawn tomorrow your friend will be a squatter and it's within my rights to have the law remove him from my land. And believe me, Arkansas Smith, we do things the correct way around here. When I come to McCord's place I will have the law right beside me. And that law will enforce my legal and proper entitlement to McCord's place.'

'A law you control.'

'On the contrary, Lance said. 'A law that does what's right. We don't want the likes of you and your friend around here. This place is intended for good people to live, not drifters like you. Nor, for that matter, small-time sod busters like McCord.'

Arkansas allowed his eyes to scan each and every man present before settling back on John Lance. To a man they fidgeted when his eyes fell on them and the tension in the air seemed to thicken somewhat.

He shifted in his saddle and shook his head.

'I plan to get Sheriff Hackman to arrest you for conspiracy to murder,' Arkansas said. 'And then I'm going to bring charges of forgery, land grabbing and attempted murder.' Arkansas leaned forward on his horse and again pointed a finger directly at John Lance. 'I'm going to ensure you hang, John Lance. You'll swing from the hemp like the common thief you are.'

The men laughed at that, but the look of sheer

116

malevolence they received from their boss stilled their hilarity. Lance's complexion had turned redder than the approaching sunset and his eyes blazed like the fires of hell itself. He had to bite down hard on his lip to keep himself under control.

'You're on my land now,' Lance said. 'And I don't take to saddle bums coming around with all sort of fancy accusations. Go now and take your gibberish with you or—'

Arkansas stopped him once again in mid speech. 'Or what?' he snarled.

Things may have progressed further at that point; it seemed that gunplay was inevitable, but then Arkansas saw a woman come out of the ranch house and stand on the boardwalk, looking puzzled at the mêlée before her.

Arkansas recognized her immediately as Rebecca.

'Daddy?' she said, in that drawl of hers and stepped down onto the dirt. She came closer to John Lance and then stopped dead when she saw Arkansas, their eyes locked and a look of sheer incomprehension crossed her face. For a moment it seemed as if she was about to say something, but no words came forth and the look of confusion on her face intensified.

Daddy! She was Lance's daughter!

Arkansas felt his stomach churn. A sharp stabbing pain in his chest that he didn't fully understand followed this. He shook his head to clear his befuddled mind but it did no good. He was stunned and felt as if a ten-pound hammer had struck him. The feelings disturbed him and the sight of Rebecca standing there stirred up conflicting emotions.

Without saying another word he turned his horse and galloped back the way he had come.

SEVENTEEN

John Lance crossed the room and placed the oil lamp on the mantel. He rubbed his hands down his trousers and looked at Jake, his foreman.

'Get Jim in here,' he said. Since the man had returned earlier he had not had a chance to speak to him, what with Arkansas Smith and then having to explain the situation to his daughter.

'Sure thing,' Jake said, and crossed the room in three massive strides.

Lance was left alone for a moment and he leaned on the mantel and stared into the flames of the fire, reflecting on the day just gone. After Arkansas had left earlier, tearing off across the grasslands like the devil was on his tail, Rebecca had come to her father, wanting to know what was happening. Apparently she knew Arkansas and had been visiting McCord's place, helping the old man who, she said, had been shot by rustlers.

That revelation had resulted in a fierce row between father and daughter.

Lance had forbidden his daughter to have anything further to do with Arkansas Smith and William McCord. She had stormed off, not understanding her father's reasoning, and it had taken some time for him to talk her round. He'd convinced her that McCord was gulching on a deal: that he'd sold his spread fair and square and had now had second thoughts and was claiming the sale never occurred; that the bill of sale was a forgery.

The entrance of the two men broke his reverie. Jim came in first with Jake following behind. The big man closed the door and stood in front of it, huge arms crossed before his impressive chest.

'You wanted to see me?' Jim asked. He wore his nervousness like a loud shirt and he gulped audibly as John Lance's eyes burned into him. If it weren't for the fact that Lance's daughter was asleep upstairs Jim would have feared for his life.

Lance nodded and took a cigar from the box. He bit off the end and spat it into the fire before taking a match to it and swallowing a mouthful of the sweet tasting tobacco.

'Tell me about Doc Cooter,' Lance said, and reclined in the soft chair beside the fire. He drew on the cigar and crossed one leg over the other, waiting.

Jim gulped once more. He didn't sit down and almost leapt out of his skin when he heard footsteps behind him, but he relaxed when he turned and saw Jake. They were old friends and he knew the big man wouldn't do him any harm.

'We just wanted to find out if McCord was alive or

dead, boss,' Jim said, trying to keep his voice firm and even but mostly failing. 'For you – because you'd asked us and we didn't know. It was an accident. We tried to scare him and the gun misfired.'

'I told you to go straight to Bowen's place.' Lance said, his voice dripping with menace, but on a sonic scale barely more than a whisper. 'Not go off looking for the doctor.'

Jim nodded. He decided against telling him that the doc was already dead before they had been ordered to go to the old Bowen place. 'We thought you'd want to know. We didn't mean to kill him.'

'What happened to Clay?'

Jim looked his boss firm in the eye and started to speak, but his words tripped over his tongue, which felt like a dry rag in his mouth.

'Well?' Lance prompted.

'He's dead.'

'I know that,' Lance said. 'Arkansas implied you shot him.'

'I weren't aiming for him,' Jim said, as if that explained everything. 'I was looking to take that Arkansas fella down but Clay came into my line of fire at the last moment. I couldn't do anything about it.'

'I see.' Lance placed the cigar in an ashtray and steepled his fingers to his lips. 'You weren't aiming for him! You killed the doc by accident and you weren't aiming for Clay! Seems you have a lot of accidents.'

Jim shrugged his shoulders and had to tense to stop his trembling knees from knocking together. His mouth was as dry as the hinges of hell and he just

121

couldn't work up any spit. He had to keep telling himself that he was safe, that they wouldn't do anything with Rebecca asleep upstairs.

They wouldn't hurt him – not here, not now.

'You've caused me some problems.'

'I'm sorry, boss.' Jim's voice broke and he lost control. 'Let me go get this Arkansas now,' he pleaded, 'I'll kill him for you.'

'Yes,' Lance said, and then nodded at Jake.

Before Jim could react, Jake's powerful hands grabbed his throat and started to squeeze. The pressure would allow nothing more than a muted gurgle to escape rom Jim's lips and he kicked and scrambled wildly. He dug his nails into Jake's hands, tearing the flesh, but the big man didn't seem to feel a thing. He pulled at the man's grip as he felt himself being lifted from his feet. His eyes pushed at their sockets and felt as if they would burst free in a splash of optic fluid. The pressure on his throat increased and he started to feel light-headed as the last of the oxygen in his body was used up. It was at that last moment of life that Jim locked eyes with John Lance and he saw only a demonic coldness.

It was a slow and painful way to die, but it was the way Jim went and it was some time before Jake released his grip and the cowboy's lifeless body fell to the floor with the hollow thud that only a dead body could make.

Lance shook his head, but before he could say a single word the door opened and Rebecca stood in the doorway. She looked first at her father and then at

Jake and then her eyes fell onto Jim's lifeless body.

Rebecca opened her mouth and screamed.

'I knew you was law,' Rycot said, and smiled so widely that the only teeth he had were visible. 'I knew it from the start. A man on the willow don't strut around like no damned rooster.'

'You calling me a chicken again?' Arkansas said, and smiled.

He had just finished telling Will and Rycot of the day and of what he'd learned. The only thing he had left out was that Rebecca was Lance's daughter; that bit of knowledge was still gnawing away at his insides. He was angrier with her than he had any right to be. The fact that she had been around on the pretence of helping Will recover while secretly getting information for her father made him madder than a drunken Indian. His feeling made him feel foolish and dented his pride somewhat; he hadn't thought he was the type to let a woman get to him like this.

He had concluded his story by showing Will and Rycot – though he doubted the livery stable man was lettered – the telegram from the Justice O'Keefe which outlined the legal standing of Arkansas Smith as a special government marshal.

'And another man has died today,' Will said, in a cold, matter-of-fact way.

'Yeah,' Arkansas said and thought of Clay. 'And there'll likely be more before all this is over.'

'So what happens next?' Will asked.

'I think Lance will be here with his so-called legal

papers in the morning,' Arkansas said. 'He'll have the
sheriff and a few hastily sworn in deputies with him,
no doubt. But what they don't realize is I can overrule
the sheriff.'

Will smiled. 'They're going to be spitting teeth over
this.'

Arkansas smiled. 'I expect so,' he said. 'And even
more so when I order the sheriff to jail Lance to await
trial by Justice O'Keefe.'

'Lance won't stand for that,' Rycot said.

'He'll have no choice,' Arkansas said firmly. 'My
evidence is flimsy and it'll come down to my word
against his, but I think the law will take my side. I've
already started the ball rolling and Justice O'Keefe is
looking into all the land deals Lance has made over
the last few years.'

'I know a few people Lance has cheated out of their
spreads,' Rycot pointed out and lit himself a cigarette.
'He's an empire builder is what he is. And he doesn't
care who he hurts to get what he wants.'

'That's true,' Will said. 'The land around here is
thin soiled. Only suitable for grazing and to make
serious money in the cattle business you need
thousands of acres. Guess that's what Lance is trying to
do.'

Arkansas took the water from the stove and poured
three cups of coffee. He handed one to both Will and
Rycot and took his own and went and stood over by
the window.

Was that the reasoning behind all this? He
wondered. Was Lance merely empire building? Was it

124

sheer greed that drove him to try and buy up every spread around the area? And what if folk refused, if his money couldn't entice them to move? Would he then try and persuade them with a gun? It certainly looked that way with Will whose land seemed to have no worth other than the actual land value, which wasn't a great deal at the moment. And old man Bowen's disappearance was still very much a mystery.

'I reckon we'd best all get some rest,' Arkansas said, and peered out of the window at the inky black landscape. 'We're all gonna need our wits about us come morning.'

'I'm fit enough to handle a gun,' Will said, and stood up as if to prove the point. There was still some pain in his side, but overall he guessed he was doing OK everything considered.

Arkansas nodded. Even although it had been little more than a flesh wound Will's recovery was remarkable. The fever, which had sapped his strength, seemed to have all but vanished.

Showed how strong he still was: once a Ranger always a Ranger.

'Never been one for shooting myself,' Rycot said. 'But if a target's big enough I can sure hit it. Might not always kill it, but I'll slow it down some.'

'Let's hope it doesn't come to that,' Arkansas said, though he knew that wasn't very likely.

He was hoping that things would start to unravel when he showed his papers to the sheriff and Lance realized he couldn't hide behind the law. Maybe Lance wouldn't have any fight in him when he knew he'd be unable to use the law to justify his crimes. It was easy enough to do all manner of ill when a man knew the law wasn't going to intervene.

'It will,' Will said, matter-of-factly. 'The only way to get a skunk like John Lance to listen is with red-hot lead.'

Arkansas turned and looked at his old partner and an understanding passed between them. They both knew that whatever morning brought them then bloodshed would be a part of it.

That much was inevitable.

'Well, we'll be ready for them,' Arkansas said.

'We'll be outnumbered,' Rycot interjected, nervously.

'My Colts are six-shooters and the Spencer takes seven. That'll be enough,' Arkansas told him, and turned his attention back to the window and the rapidly retreating night outside. Dawn would be here in a matter of a few hours and with it would come the day of reckoning. 'We'd best get some sleep now.'

'Who can sleep with all this going on?' Rycot paced the room, as jumpy as a tick on a hot plate. 'Damn, couldn't sleep if I tried.' He continued to pace and when he got no answer he turned and noticed the other two men were indeed fast asleep. Will was slumped in the soft chair and Arkansas was curled in the foetal position on the floor.

He shook his head in wonder. He couldn't understand how these men could switch off so easily. Come dawn, Lance and his men would turn up, armed to the teeth and bloodshed would surely follow. And yet these two men were sleeping away as if they didn't have a care in the world. He shook his head again and crept slowly over to the table and grabbed the remainder of the whiskey before sitting himself down in a corner.

EIGHTEEN

'Here they come,' Arkansas warned and worked a slug into the chamber of the Spencer. He looked at Will and Rycot and nodded for them to take up their positions, which they did with the minimum of fuss.

They had been preparing for this since first light. The plan had been talked over in great detail – when Lance and his men arrived Arkansas was going to go out to meet them, while Will would take up position at the window, rifle ready should anyone go for their guns. Rycot would stand in the doorway, his ancient but reliable rifle offering further deterrent against trouble.

Arkansas felt that John Lance didn't have the stomach for real trouble and would be unlikely to provoke a gunfight if there was the slightest chance of him getting hurt. He would have no compulsion about killing them all if it suited his needs, but he would much rather get others to carry out his killing while he remained at a safe distance. As it was none of them wanted to have to use their weapons, but it didn't hurt to let the opposition know what they were up against.

'How many?' Will asked, straining his eyes to make out the men coming down the slope above the valley.

'I count maybe ten men,' Arkansas said. 'We'll know soon enough.'

'I recognize the sheriff,' Rycot said. 'I know that long coat he wears. And that's John Lance beside him. I'd know that arrogant, smug, son of a bitch anywhere. Could spot him a hundred miles away in a snowstorm if both my eyeballs had been poked out and their lids stitched together.'

As the men neared, it became evident that both Arkansas and Rycot had been correct in their guesses. Lance rode up front, the sheriff behind him while eight other men, all armed, wearing gunbelts as well as carrying rifles, the butts protruding from the saddle boots, came just behind them. They looked like a well-armed militia and were obviously intending to intimidate.

Arkansas stepped out onto boardwalk and coolly waited for them. He left the Spencer leaning in the open doorway but within easy reach. At close range he was quicker and far more effective with his six-shooters in any case, but it wouldn't hurt to have the rifle should the need arise.

Lance smiled when he saw Arkansas and he brought his horse to a halt a few feet from the man. The sheriff pulled up level beside him and the rest of the men remained behind but spread themselves out in a straight line either side of their boss.

Arkansas had to give them credit. They certainly knew what they were doing; spread out like that they gave the impression of numbering more than they truly were. They were a formidable looking bunch even without the military tactics.

'You know what I've come for,' John Lance said, addressing his words at Arkansas.

'Remind me,' Arkansas replied, speaking to Lance but looking directly at the sheriff who shifted uncomfortably in his saddle. He quickly looked to his left as he saw the end of Will's rifle protrude out through the gap in the window. Will was making sure the men knew he was there but offering as small a target as possible. His years with the Rangers had not been forgotten.

John Lance shook his head and spat onto the ground. 'Show him the papers.'

The sheriff reached into his coat pocket and brought out a legal-looking document. It was rolled into a tube and secured by a red ribbon. 'This proves that John Lance is now the rightful owner of this property,' he said, and had to clear his throat. 'We intend to take possession here and now.'

'Can I see that?' Arkansas asked, and stepped closer to the sheriff.

'Sure.' The sheriff dismounted and then held the document out.

Arkansas reached out and took the document from him, opened it and then it was his turn to shake his head. 'I don't believe this is genuine,' he said, though he had to admit to himself that Will's signature looked real enough. Whoever had done the forging they were certainly a master of their craft. Maybe that was why Will's place had been ransacked the night he had been shot, he thought. Perhaps Lance's men were looking for an example of Will's signature someone could copy. It was a damn fine forgery in any case.

He walked over to the window and held the document against the glass. 'You recognize this?'

'Ain't never seen it before,' Will answered.

Arkansas walked back over and stood before the open door. He smiled at Rycot who was standing there, pointing his rifle directly at John Lance, but his legs were shaking slightly.

'As I say,' Arkansas said, 'I don't believe this is genuine.'

'It's genuine,' Lance said, with much venom in his voice. With his private army spread out around him he seemed to possess a confidence that had not been evident earlier. He looked at his men each side of him with an exaggerated turn of the head, as if reminding Arkansas that they were there and that he was hopelessly outnumbered. 'Don't make us use our guns,' he warned.

'We don't want trouble,' the sheriff said, quickly, hoping to diffuse the situation. 'But I must tell you it is my legal duty to see that McCord is evicted and that the law is served.'

'I believe I'll keep these documents,' Arkansas said, and rolled them back up, secured the ribbon and placed them into his pocket. 'Now I've got papers also.'

'What is this?' John Lance asked. He bit his lip in anticipation and stared at the man called Arkansas Smith.

Arkansas pulled one of the telegrams he had received only days ago from his jacket and coolly walked over and handed it to the sheriff.

Arkansas stood there, hands hanging at his sides with thumbs facing inwards towards his guns while he waited for the reaction he knew would surely come.

There was confusion. Lance looked across at the sheriff and then leaned over in the saddle and snatched the papers from him. He read through them several times before speaking.

'What manner of joke is this?' he asked, and then read the papers yet again as if willing the words contained there to disappear. His face went a vivid crimson and his eyes narrowed to slits.

'Now, Sheriff,' Arkansas said, 'I require the arrest of John Lance. And when the justice arrives he can make a ruling on this so-called sale. I'll be bringing charges of murder, forgery and whatever else I can dig up on Mister John Lance.'

'Are you going to stand for this?' Lance said, waving the telegram about. He glared at the sheriff. 'These papers don't mean anything. How do we know they are genuine?' He crumpled the telegram and threw it onto the ground next to Arkansas who bent and smoothed them out before returning them to his pocket.

'I'm sorry,' Sheriff Hackman said, looking at John Lance 'There's nothing I can do here. That telegram's from the Territorial Governor's office and the orders came there from Washington. I'm being ordered to take orders from this man.' He pointed to Arkansas who smirked at Lance.

'What is this?' Lance screamed. 'McCord sold this place and now he's trying to back down on the deal.'

'This is bigger than you and me,' Hackman said, and gave Lance a timid look.

Lance's men grew visibly nervous and it seemed that any moment now they would start shooting. They didn't completely understand what was happening here. What had been written on the paper Arkansas had shown the sheriff? They held back, but each and every one of them was like a coiled spring.

Will opened the window and looked Lance directly in the eye before speaking. 'I wouldn't sell anything to you,' he said. 'Now get off my land.' He pushed the eye of his rifle out of the window and squared it directly at the rancher.

'Sheriff' – Lance turned to the sheriff – 'you can't side with these men. I demand you do your duty, or I'll do it for you.'

'I ain't siding with anyone,' Hackman said. 'I got no choice here. Those orders, John. They come from the Presidential office. Do you understand that?'

'You work for me,' Lance screamed, which made the sheriff wince.

'John,' the sheriff said. He knew Lance's temper would get the better of him and there was no telling where this would go now. It was all an unknown to him and he wasn't qualified to guess. He was just a small town sheriff and those papers he had seen had come from the top. There was no higher.

The wise thing to do would be to go along with this Arkansas Smith and see what developed, try and figure a way out later when they'd all had a chance to better consider their options. Only that wasn't going to happen. John Lance was too used to getting his own way and would stir up a whirlwind when things didn't go in a fashion that suited him.

'You work for me!' Lance repeated, yelling wildly. His eyes burnt with feral intent and he pulled his lips back in a snarl over gritted teeth.

'The sheriff is supposed to work for the law,' Arkansas said. 'If he can't do that he ain't worth a damn and I'll have his badge here and now.'

'Look, John' – the sheriff stared Lance directly in the eyes – 'we'll do what this fella says for now. We can prove your innocence of all this when the judge arrives. For now we've got no choice but to comply with this man's orders. You read the telegram.'

'Get off your horse,' Arkansas ordered, 'and relinquish your firearms. I'm arresting you as is my right under the special powers invested in me by the President.' Behind him he heard Rycot let out a small chuckle. The events seemed to have brightened up his day no end.

'Do as he says,' the sheriff again pleaded. 'It's the only way, John. We've got no choice.'

'I own you,' Lance snarled.

Suddenly, before anyone could react, Lance produced a highly polished derringer from his sleeve and shot the sheriff directly in the chest. The .410 slug was deadly effective at such close range and the sheriff's chest opened up in a burst of crimson spray as he was thrown backwards to come down hard against the cabin wall.

The sheriff slid to the ground and he looked down at his bloodstained shirt in disbelief. He brought a hand to the wound as if willing it to not be there.

'You shot me,' he said, incredulously.

John Lance fought to keep his horse under control and he stared back at the sheriff as if not believing himself what had just happened.

'You shot me!' the sheriff said again. Somehow he'd always known his association with John Lance would end this way. He cursed the day he had first met the rancher. Then he felt a tremendous wave of pain, but also a great feeling of release, as his heart slowly ground to a halt.

With that he was dead.

Lance fired the derringer again, but this time he was aiming at Arkansas.

It was then that all hell broke loose.

NINETEEN

Between the second explosion from the derringer and the sheriff being thrown backwards time seemed to stand still.

Arkansas heard the click of guns as triggers were squeezed and hammers pulled back. He pulled his own Colt from leather and let off a wild shot before leaping for the doorway.

He collided with Rycot and both men tumbled to the floor.

Arkansas rolled and kicked the door closed just as the wood splintered and a bullet screamed past his head. It had been so close that he had felt the air warm up as it went on its way into the wall behind him with a burst of dust and splinters.

Will was at the window, firing with the rifle through the opening. He let off two shots and then turned quickly away from the window just in time as the glass exploded and shards went every which way. Immediately he worked the action of the rifle and turned back to the window, hit the remainder of the glass out and fired again.

'Got one,' he said and watched a man thrown backwards off his panicked horse.

The flimsily built cabin was scant protection against the onslaught of bullets and holes suddenly appeared in the walls, sending tiny splinters onto the air. Arkansas got to his feet, checked Rycot. He was fine, other than being terrified.

Arkansas ran towards the window. Again fortune shone on him and another bullet tore through the wall and passed by even closer than the last. It had been so close he could have shaken hands with it and wished it well on its merry way.

He got to the window and grinned at Will.

'Just like old times,' he said, and quickly fired through the window. One of his shots found a target and he saw a man throw up his arms and slide from his startled horse. His legs got tangled up in the saddle and the galloping horse dragged him, but he didn't seem to mind any seeing as he was already dead. The second shot went wide of a mark.

Outside Lance's men returned fire and Will and Arkansas had to fall to the floor and lay prone while bullets passed through the walls as if they were butter. Rycot still hadn't got up from the floor and he could see no reason to bother at the present moment.

'This ain't good,' Rycot yelled, but the roar of gunfire drowned his words out. He buried his face in the floor and placed his arms over his head as wood splinters and lead flew overhead. If he ever saw hell then he was sure that this was pretty much what it would be like.

'You OK?' Arkansas asked.

With a grimace, Will rolled onto his back and started reloading the rifle.

'Never felt better,' he yelled. 'Forgotten how good it felt to have a damn good fight.'

'Good? This ain't what I call good,' Rycot yelled. The old man was obviously better suited to tending horses than battling gunmen. 'You two is plumb loco if you're asking me.'

A large section of the door imploded as someone outside let off a shotgun.

'Ready?' Arkansas nodded at Will.

'Yeah,' Will said. 'But just help me up.'

They both understood each other and the tactic they were about to try was second nature to them. They had done it so many times in the past that neither needed to outline their plans to the other.

Arkansas reached out and grabbed Will beneath his arm. They both got to their knees and knelt besides the window.

'After three,' Arkansas said, and held tighter beneath his friend's arm. 'One.'

A bullet smashed into a picture on the wall behind and it fell to the floor.

'Two.'

Rycot's whimpering grew louder and he positively screamed as the shotgun blew in a large section of the wall.

'Three . . .'

The two men came upright as one and both started

shooting from their respective positions, neither of them aimed but instead shot repeatedly in opposite directions before, still shooting, and screaming like banshees they each brought their aim towards dead centre. As they moved they created a wide line of fire and the men outside had to pull back.

Arkansas had emptied one of the Colts and Will had used up all seven his rifle had to offer. Arkansas let off three shots in quick succession while Will reloaded and then as soon as the older man had resumed firing through the window, he ducked back and reloaded both Colts.

'We got them on the run,' Will yelled, delight evident in his voice. He was enjoying each and every moment of the chaos that surrounded him.

Throughout all this Rycot felt it prudent to remain hugging the floorboards, but he reconsidered when a bullet kicked up dust from the floor only inches away from his left leg. He yelped and with surprising agility got to his feet and ran across to the bedroom.

'They're running,' Will whooped with delight. 'We scared them away.' He let off a shot for good luck and in the distance saw another of Lance's men fall from his horse.

'We spanked them good,' Rycot said, and emerged from the bedroom. He ran over to the window and peered at what looked like a battlefield. After the chaos of only moments ago everything was eerily silent. 'How many of the varmints did we get?'

'If any of them are hiding in the bedroom,' Arkansas said, 'I'm sure you got them good.'

He walked over to the door and went outside with Will and Rycot following closely behind.

'Four of them,' Rycot said. 'We got four of them.'

'Five more dead,' Will said, and looked down at the sheriff.

The lawman looked back at him from lifeless eyes.

There were three more men dead outside the cabin and another body could be seen some thirty feet away where he had finally fallen from his terrified horse.

John Lance didn't appear to be among the slain.

In the distance, a thick dust cloud could be seen, thrown up by the retreat of Lance and his men. Considering only ten minutes or so ago they had been so keen to take possession of this place, they were sure in a damn hurry to get away.

'What you going to do now?' Will asked, feeding fresh shells into his rifle.

Arkansas allowed his eyes to drift over the battlefield his friend's land had become. Five men killed here today and he knew there would be more before all this was over. And for what? So John Lance could own a little more land than he already owned, so that he could put his name to yet another spread. It was all a senseless waste and it made Arkansas sick to the stomach.

If the West was ever going to become a safe and decent place to live, to raise a family, to run a business, then people like John Lance had to be eliminated and taken out of the running. If this new United States of America was ever to prosper and realize its full potential then John Lance, and others of his kind, had

140

to be removed from the foundations before greatness could be built.

When Arkansas Smith had escaped that hangman's noose back in Reno it became his duty to eradicate the John Lances of this world.

'I've got to go after Lance,' he said, and bent and pulled the star from the sheriff's shirt. He pinned it on his own chest and rolled and lit a quirly. 'Guess this means I'm the law around here. Least for the moment.'

TWENTY

Will insisted on going with Arkansas. He'd been fine during the battle of only moments ago and, he pointed out; he'd had worse injuries than this gut wound which had all but healed in any case. Rycot, on the other hand, insisted on riding back into town and passing on the news of the sheriff's murder. He'd then get up a group of the town's men and bring them out to Lance's place to assist in the arrest of the varmint.

Arkansas, in no mood to argue with either man, simply nodded.

They had then rounded up one of the dead men's horses and Will had groaned as he mounted it, but he managed to do so without any assistance. He clutched his stomach and took several deep breaths.

'I'll be fine,' he said. 'Ain't nothing more than a dull ache.'

'Come on then,' Arkansas said and turned the sorrel. He looked back over his shoulder at Rycot who was standing beside the sheriff's body. 'Take his weapons back into town. Let folk know what happened and start looking for a new sheriff.'

Rycot nodded. He was eager to get going, having experienced enough action for one day.

One entire lifetime, for that matter.

'You ready now?' Will asked. 'At this rate Lance will have died of old age before we get to him.'

'Sure,' Arkansas said, and slid his Spencer into the saddle boot.

'Just like old times,' Will said with a smile, and then, as he had so many times in the past, he brought a hand down hard on his horse's rump and yelled, 'Rangers ride!'

'Like old times.' Arkansas agreed and spurred the sorrel into a gallop.

As soon as they reached his ranch John Lance had ordered Jake, his foreman, to get every man who could shoot armed up with a rifle and six-gun, and ready for Arkansas Smith when he came riding in.

He wanted the man dead.

Whatever else happened he wanted that man dead.

Then he had gone straight into the house where Rebecca confronted him. He hadn't seen much of her since the incident with Jim. She'd run to her room and refused to speak to him and at the time that had pretty much suited him. She didn't understand what had to be done in business. There were men who would trample a weak man and take everything he owned. This was a savage land and the only way to prosper was to constantly expand, and building respect from fear did that.

143

Rebecca looked at him and from his agitated manner she could see that he was troubled.

'What have you done now?' she asked.

'Leave it,' he commanded and made to go past her but she stood defiant and blocked his way.

'I won't,' she said. 'Last night a man was killed in this house, murdered at your orders. Now what have you done?'

'Daughter, I am telling you to stand aside.'

'No,' Rebecca said. Last night things had changed between them and they would never be the same again. In fact she had already made up her mind. She was leaving, turning her back on her father and the past. She would never return.

'Move.' Firm. Lance looked at his daughter in a way he never had before.

She shook her head.

Lance brought up a hand and slapped his daughter so hard that she was knocked off her feet. He grabbed her by the back of her hair and pulled her, protesting all the way, up the stairs and across the landing to her room. He kicked the door open and then threw her, sobbing, onto the bed.

'I'll speak to you later,' he said and closed and locked the door.

Lance ran back down the stairs and went into the large dining-room at the rear of the ranch house. He grabbed a bottle of whiskey from the cabinet and tore the cork stopper free. He took a large gulp straight from the bottle and took it with him back into the small room that served as his home office.

He went to the window and looked out to see that Jake had gathered together over a dozen men. He counted thirteen in all. He took another huge gulp from the whiskey and then stumbled out into the hall. Once there he paused to take down his Sharps carbine from the wall and then went outside.

'Men,' he yelled and swayed on his feet. 'I'll give a one hundred-dollar bonus to the man who kills Arkansas Smith.'

'We'll get him, Mister Lance,' Jake said. 'Don't you worry none about that.'

'I won't worry,' Lance said. He was starting to slur his words and he had to hold onto the doorframe to stop himself from falling. He took yet another drink of the whiskey and then wiped his lips on the back of the sleeve.

'I want that bastard dead!' he yelled.

'We'll get him,' Jake repeated and then raised his hands for the men to cheer in support. They had to get Lance inside. Like this, he would be a liability when a fight started and more likely to kill himself than anyone else.

'Good,' Lance said, and punched the air. For a moment it looked as if he was going to fall over but then he squinted his eyes and pointed. 'Look, here they come.'

Jake looked over his shoulder and sure enough he saw the men coming. They were riding at speed across the flatlands that led up to Lance's ranch.

There were only two of them: they were vastly outnumbered.

145

'Kill the bastards,' John Lance yelled, and then disappeared back into the ranch house.

TWENTY-ONE

Lance's ranch house was a large grand-looking structure, built with a mixture of Spanish and English influences. The lower section of the wall was made from adobe blocks but the upper sections were constructed from local lumber. There was a sloping roof on the main ranch house but the outbuildings, although sharing the same basic style, were flat-roofed.

It was not the best place meet an enemy since there were too many places where a man could remain concealed. Arkansas knew this from his previous visit and he slowed his horse almost to a halt just before he got into rifle range.

He motioned for Will to do likewise.

'How many men do you think we're up against?' Will asked.

Arkansas squinted against the sun glare and stared at the sprawling ranch house and its surrounding buildings. It looked quiet – deserted, but he knew that would not be the case. No doubt Lance's men were concealed, waiting to catch them in a deadly crossfire as they rode in.

'Your guess is as good as mine.'

'It's a shame we ain't got more men,' Will said, and then took the makings from his shirt and rolled and lit a quirly. He blew a thick stream of smoke out between his teeth before asking, 'How do you want to play this?'

'Can I have some of that Durham?' Arkansas asked, ignoring the question, and leaned across and took the leather pouch from his friend. He skilfully constructed a smoke and took a sulphur match to it.

For a few moments they sat there, smoking and watching the Lance place. Still there was no movement. The place shimmered in the late morning sunshine and could very well have been a painting for all the movement evident. Even the landscape surrounding it seemed to be as still as an artist's impression.

'Remember that time we went up against Jack Giles's gang?' Arkansas asked.

'Sure do.' Will nodded and flicked the remains of his quirly away. 'Down in Lincoln.'

'Well, there were nine of them and we're still here. They ain't.'

Jack Giles and his gang had been terrorizing folk along the Santa Fe Trail, robbing and murdering with seeming impunity from the law. There had been nine of them that night in Lincoln when the two Texas Rangers rode in in search of one of the gang members who was wanted back in Texas for the murder of a sheriff. As Arkansas had said it had been nine against two and yet when the dust had settled and the cordite cleared from the air it was only the two Rangers who remained standing.

'And you want to handle this the same way?'

'Pretty much,' Arkansas said. 'We'll take the fight to them. They won't be expecting that. Then we get down behind cover as soon as possible. Then we've got a chance of spotting who we're up against.'

'You ain't forgot your Ranger training,' Will said, with a wry smile. He had that old feeling that pre-empted a battle, that mix of adrenaline and fear. It made him feel alive.

'Once a Ranger,' Arkansas said with a grin, 'always a Ranger.'

Without another word they moved off at a slow trot towards the ranch house. They were both ready to set their horses off in opposite directions should a shot ring out. Each knew what the other would be thinking and they operated as a single entity, joined by their shared experiences of all the times they had faced certain death together and triumphed. They were each an extension of the other and both moved like the well-oiled workings of a revolver.

'After three,' Arkansas said.

They each slid their rifles from their respective saddle boots and took the reins of their horses tight in one hand.

'One.'

The two men looked at each other for a moment and nodded their understanding.

'Two.'

They led their horses apart so that although side-by-side, they had in fact increased the space between them.

'Three . . .' Arkansas said, let off a shot and, taking the reins in his teeth, filled his free hand with a Colt and started galloping in a zigzag fashion towards Lance's place.

Will did likewise and between them they kept the hot lead flying.

Fire was returned, but both Arkansas and Will made difficult targets as they jostled back and forth on their horses. It was Arkansas who reached the gates to the stockade first and he brought the sorrel into a jump that easily cleared the fence. Will came in directly behind him but his horse clipped the fence and the beast landed awkwardly, sending him crashing to the hard ground.

Arkansas brought his horse to a sudden halt and let off several shots towards one of the barns and jumped from his horse and ran to his friend. Dust spat up around him as each bullet got that little bit closer than the one before. He saw movement out of the corner of his eye and he turned and shot, just in time to see one of Lance's men scream and fall forward from the roof of the ranch house.

First blood.

Arkansas reached Will and grabbed him beneath the arm. Together they ran across the courtyard and dived for cover behind the privy.

'We're in the shit now,' Will said, and Arkansas was

glad to see his friend had not lost his sense of humour.

'Never did get used to your jokes.'

Gunfire seemed to come from all directions and sections of the privy wall suddenly disappeared. Arkansas said a silent prayer and then came out of concealment and fired the Colt in the direction he thought the firing was coming from. He caught sight of a man as he peered out from behind the smallest of the three barns to his left and he fired. His shot was true and the man suddenly threw his arms up as the back of his head exploded onto the wall behind him.

Arkansas dived for the relative safety of the privy.

'I got another one.'

'We need to get behind them,' Will said. 'See that fence? Should be able to see a target from there.' He pointed to the corral fence that ran alongside the barn. Beyond it there was an area of greenery where someone had started a garden.

Arkansas nodded. 'You cover me.'

Will nodded. 'Go,' he yelled and emerged from cover himself. He worked the action of the Spencer like the old pro he was and he was only vaguely aware of his friend running behind him. He let off the last of the rifle's seven and dived back for cover just as a bullet came so close that it took out the heel of one of his boots. He quickly reloaded.

'Not bad for an old-timer,' Arkansas shouted back with a cheeky grin and fired off a shot at a man who moments ago had been concealed from view but was now visible beside the porch of the house. The man didn't even know what hit him and he fell down dead,

151

a hole straight between the eyes.

Arkansas had to hug the ground when fire came at him from the roof of the barn. Holding a hand over his head he chanced a look upwards and he saw the large man who had been at Will's place with Lance earlier. He noticed Will take down another man who had run out of cover and was trying to rush the old Ranger, but he just wasn't quick enough.

The man on the roof started running, vanishing from Arkansas's view for a moment. But Arkansas pre-empted the man's plan. And as soon as he appeared at the other side of the barn, directly above him, and popped his head out for a shot Arkansas blew it clean off.

John Lance suddenly appeared in the doorway of the ranch house and took a startled look around. He had a rifle in one hand and a half-drunk bottle of whiskey in the other. He pulled the trigger of the rifle and sent a bullet up through his porch.

'Kill the bastards,' he yelled, slurring his words. He downed another mouthful of the whiskey and then threw the bottle across the yard. He lifted the rifle and fired wildly at nothing in particular and then vanished back inside the house.

'Hold your fire,' someone shouted and then emerged from behind the barn, his arms held high. He was followed by another man, then another and. . . .

Silence fell.

It was over.

Now all that remained was to get John Lance.

TWENTY-TWO

Arkansas and Will had disarmed the remaining five men, but there was no need; they weren't going to fight further. Whatever this war was about, they had decided they wanted no further part in it. Jake was dead and they'd just seen their boss acting like a lunatic. There was no reason to fight on.

Will held his rifle trained on the men who, as instructed, were seated, hands under their rumps, against the barn.

Suddenly the peace was ripped apart when all the windows in lower storey of the ranch house exploded and orange flames followed to lick angrily at the air outside.

'Mr Lance is in there,' someone shouted.

'Let the skunk burn,' Will said. 'He's responsible for all this. It's no more than he deserves and will save the town the cost of a trial.'

Arkansas looked at the ranch house. The flames had completely taken hold and the fire engulfed the lower floors. He wasn't sure how it had started –

perhaps a stray bullet had struck an oil lamp inside the house causing the fire to start and spread rapidly. He thought of John Lance, trapped, consumed by the fire. The suddenly he thought of Rebecca. With everything that had been going on he hadn't given her much thought.

Was she in there?

'I'm going in,' he said and threw down his own rifle. He ran across the courtyard and struck the ranch house door hard with a shoulder. The door gave and when he got to his feet it was as if he could have entered the gates of hell itself.

The room to his left was completely engulfed and he felt his eyes sear as he looked into the raging inferno. Everything else was shrouded in a dense cloud of smoke and he had to cover his mouth with the back of his hand and breathe as little as possible.

He could just make out the stairs in front of him and he ran for them. He reached them and had just started up when he felt someone come at him from behind and before he could do anything about it he was pushed to the floor. He hit hard, the wind pushing from his lungs. He felt his attacker's hands going for his throat and he brought up his own to break the grasp.

It was John Lance and Arkansas could see madness in his eyes as he tried to push him off. At that moment he realized the man was insane and that he had set this fire himself. He intended to burn along with his empire.

He heard screaming from one of the bedrooms.

Rebecca.

Wherever she was she was unable to get out.

Arkansas tried to break free of Lance but the rancher was a powerful man, doubly so in his mania and Arkansas felt light-headed from the lack of clean air. He was weak and feared that at any moment he'd pass out and burn alongside this madman. He could hear the commotion outside, as everyone had joined together to fight the fire.

They would fight in vain, though. The fire had more than a foothold.

It had a free rein.

Rebecca screamed again, frantic, sheer panic.

Arkansas found a small reserve of strength from somewhere and he managed to lift his knees and use his legs to break Lance's grip. He kicked out suddenly and Lance fell backwards, down the stairs, into the flames.

Arkansas got to his feet and ran up the remainder of the stairs and took them three at the time. The air was slightly better at the top and he took a quick gulp and ran across the landing towards the screaming.

He found the door and he tried it, but it was locked.

Lance had locked her, his own daughter, in the bedroom and then torched the place.

If ever there had been any doubt of his madness then it had long gone: the man was nothing short of a stark raving lunatic.

Arkansas went at the door with his shoulder. At first it refused to give and he pounded it three more times before the wood splintered and he was able to kick the panels in.

Rebecca came out of the room, coughing, spluttering and fell into his arms.

'Hold it.'

Arkansas turned and saw John Lance standing besides them. He had a shotgun pointed dead centre of them. Behind him the flames had followed him up the stairs and were now licking at the upper ceiling.

'Don't be a fool,' Arkansas said. 'We'll all burn to death. Is that what you want? Do you want your own daughter to die? Come on, man.'

Lance started to laugh, great bellowing guffaws. He threw his head back and roared from deep within his stomach. The shotgun waved about perilously in his hand.

At that moment Arkansas knew that he was looking into the eyes of the devil himself. Lance's brain had snapped.

There was to be no reasoning with him.

'Daddy,' Rebecca whimpered and buried her face into Arkansas's chest.

'Lance' Arkansas snapped, 'put the gun down. We'll all get out of the bedroom window. Now, before it's too late.'

For one awful moment Arkansas thought Lance was going to pull the trigger, but then they were all engulfed in a shower of sparks as the ceiling above them gave in. Arkansas couldn't be positive but moments before entering the bedroom he thought he saw the floor beneath John Lance suddenly give way and swallow the man. The rancher had fallen into the heart of the flames, consumed by an inferno of his own doing.

Arkansas dragged Rebecca across the bedroom he'd only moments ago released her from. He moved as quickly as possible to the window and kicked the glass out. It was some thirty feet to the ground below but he had no time to take care with their fall.

The air was becoming so hot that he could feel his skin blistering and Rebecca was like a rag doll in his arms. They wouldn't survive more than another few seconds before the smoke claimed them and left them for the hungry flames that would not rest until everything within its path had been consumed.

'Come on,' Arkansas said and he pulled her up onto the window ledge. 'We've got to jump.' But she was no longer hearing him. She went limp in his arms. She had fainted clean away and for the second time Arkansas held the unconscious girl in his arms.

Behind him the flames grew stronger and even hotter still. Smoke piled into the room, the broken window providing ventilation and sucking the noxious fumes out into the afternoon sky.

Arkansas held Rebecca to him and together they leapt out of the window.

That was it: it was all over.

Arkansas allowed Will to help him to his feet just in time to see one of Lance's men lead Rebecca off to one of the outbuildings. He made to go after her but Will held him back.

'They're going to take her into town,' Will said. 'With her pa gone she pretty much owns half of Red Rock now. I had no idea she was John Lance's daughter.'

Arkansas smiled and turned back to look at what was left of the ranch house. The structure had now all but succumbed to the greedy flames and, as he watched, the roof caved in and sent a shower of sparks floating into the sky. The building was totally gutted by the fire and for a moment he thought of John Lance trapped within the inferno. He'd be dead by now – no one could have survived in there.

'Can you ride?' Will asked.

Arkansas didn't think he'd picked up any major injuries in the leap from the window; just a few cuts and bruises. His left shoulder ached, but he didn't think it was broken. And he could feel swelling forming around his eyes. He coughed and gulped in the clean air.

'I'll be fine.'

'Then let's saddle up,' Will said. 'Ain't nothing more we can do here. And I suppose you can say justice has been served.'

'Of a sort,' Arkansas said. 'Of a sort.'

TWENTY-THREE

Arkansas shook Will's hand one more time and then mounted the sorrel. He adjusted his hat, pulling the brim down to shield his eyes from the fierce sun.

'I'll be seeing you.'

'Sure.' Will nodded and simply turned and walked back into his cabin. They had said their goodbyes and there was nothing more to be said. Each understood the other.

It had been a week since the fire. John Lance had perished and taken the secrets of his schemes and indeed the full extent of his crimes to the grave with him.

Arkansas hadn't seen Rebecca since they taken a tumble from the burning house that day. As far as he knew she was staying at her hotel in Red Rock for the time being. She would no doubt need to grieve before deciding on her future.

He had thought about trying to see her but had decided against it. She'd known where he was and if there were anything to be said she'd be able to find him at Will's place, but she hadn't come and now it was too late.

He took one last look around and smiled when his eyes fell on the horses in the corral. Will had claimed them from Lance's own stock, saying it was only fair compensation considering all he had been through. The wind was starting to pick up and although the sun blazed down there was the hint of a coming storm in the air. Winter wasn't that far off and was already making its presence felt.

'Come on, girl.' Arkansas patted the side of sorrel's head and set her off in a steady trot. He headed across the valley floor, towards the mountains and whatever lay beyond.

LIBRARY LINK ISSUES – For Staff Only

1	2	3	4	5	6	7	8	9
		3м						